The Beginning of the End

Saivya Singh

Invincible Publishers

First Printing: 2019

ISBN: 978-81-943134-4-1

Invincible Publishers

Registered Address: 201A, SAS Tower, Sector 38, Gurgaon - 122003

I would like to dedicate this book to "Saibaba" for being my guiding light and always showering me with his grace and blessings.

Acknowledgement

I would also like to thank my late Grand Father Sujan Singh. I know his blessings are always there with me.

I thank my Paternal Grand Mother (Mrs. Kamala Singh), and my Maternal Grand Pa (Chandrika Prasad) and my Maternal Grand Ma (Nirmala Prasad) and all my elders in my family for their Best Wishes.

I would like to take this opportunity to show my gratitude to my parents (Ms. Pratibha and Mr. Nagendra Singh) for their constant encouragement and motivation that helped me to achieve this first milestone in my life.

Last but not the least I would like to also thank "Invincible Publications" for giving me an opportunity to present my work to the community and "Special Thanks" to Ms. Pooja (The Editor) and Ms. Tamanna from Invincible Publications for their effort in getting this book published.

Table of Content

Chapter 1

"Bring the crystals to me now!" A voice boomed across the chasm, toppling various artefacts and splintering the dusty wall. The room was circular in shape with broken walls. And, different antique cupboards which were brimming with old and decaying objects. In the middle of the room, there was a huge fissure, which led to the never-ending dark abyss. There were different wisps of ghastly blood-red smoke with a tinge of bright orange choking out of the chasm with a volcanic like smell. The soldiers who stood before the Emperor stood with fearful expressions on their face. The man who was kneeling down before the Emperor had a calm expression on his face, he had green emerald eyes. He wore a mask on his face with various scars embedded on it. "I am weak now" continued the Emperor, "But as soon as I get the crystals I will regain my old form and make things right again" "I have good news for u sir" said the man in the mask, "one of the crystals is located on earth, I don't know where but I can sense it, and I will soon find out where it is and get it". "Very well then," said the Emperor "Go and get me the crystals at the earliest" the man with the mask smiled coldly under his cover and said, "It will be my pleasure" with that the man dissolved Into pure green light. The Emperor closed his fist, and with that said: "The beginning of the end is near."

Blake was having a terrible day, in P.E he accidentally smacked his nose to the wall while playing basketball, and his nose suddenly turned into a red overflowing river. Then while walking down the stairs, he "accidentally" tripped his friend Alex and was brought to the principal's office because Alex apparently had broken his arm falling down the stairs…(hey that was not his fault, Alex should have tried to break his fall or something..) So basically, Blake was the average middle school kid who did ordinary things and had an average lifestyle. But his life was about to really get not average and incredibly messed up when he was going to vanish a monster goat who had chain mail, sneakers, bling and bad attitude…

Blake was bored, he just stared at the pigeons on the tree branch swaying around in the wind, the only thing other than stare at the pigeons was to watch a bunch of goats graze in the grass, "man this school trip hike is so boring. I wish I would have never come for this hike." Blake looked at the pigeons and moaned, thankfully. The pigeons did not respond and continued to do whatever pigeons do in their free time. He left the company of the pigeons and started to walk down to his class. As he was walking, he saw one goat gazing with his storm green eyes, he found it a bit suspicious as goats do not have different color eyes, and they do not stare at humans. But, as soon as he looked back, the goat was nowhere to be seen. He found that a bit strange, but he continued to walk back to his class thinking it was his imagination. As soon as he was about to greet his teacher and give him an explanation to why he was he not with his class taking pictures of birds. And what was he doing alone near the farm with the pigeon, He felt a searing hot pain in his stomach, the impact was so powerful he got knocked back, and he fell onto the pavement. He hit his head hard on a wall, and his vision started to diminish.

Chapter 2

He slowly got up, part by part and looked around. The whole place was destroyed. The house where his class was hanging around was completely rapaciously torn by the blast. Dust was everywhere, his vision was blurry, and the pain in his stomach was feeling like a hot knife was being pressed into it, and then he saw a figure, emerging from the dust and debris. He was expecting to see a monster, or an alien or maybe even a dragon. But what he was not expecting was the same green eye goat, with a chain mail, white sneakers and black trousers with a black shirt and a leather jacket with shiny golden bling wrapped all around the goat's neck. The shirt read "This guy got GOAT swag." the goat itself was talking on the phone and seemed to pay him no attention at all, the conversation on the phone went like "ya bro, (or goat or whatever goats call their buddies) Iv Come to this location, I need to get the boy right?". Blake had a strong feeling in his gut that boy actually referred to him. "Okay, then!" The goat said, "Come here at once and ill spare ur life." "Like that's gonna happen" replied Blake. Blake charged at the monster goat with full speed. He slid on the slippery surface and accidentally somersaulted on the goat. He panicked and tried to get down, but in the process he kicked the goat in his eyes. He fell banged his head on the surface, got up, folded his arms and tried to summon a confident smile. Implying that this was all his idea and not an accident "Enough of games" said the monster goat, rubbing his eyes "I'm coming for u now," with that the goat erupted into green light and charged at Blake.

Blake was not feeling like fighting, he had already finished his portion of fighting over the weekend when he sent two boys in his class to the nurse, just yesterday… But, this goat looked pretty serious when he said he needed to get him. And he had a bad feeling that the goat had a reputation of getting things done. So when the goat charged at him, he simply knelt and screamed: "I give up, take me wherever u need!". The monster goat abruptly stopped in his tracks, and looked at Blake, he tried to give a frightened look, (he was good at drama) after about 20 seconds, the goat (clearly dissatisfied) said- "Okay then follow me, our ride will be here in about 15 mins." Blake looked down at the ground, he planned to surprise an attack on him because he knew he could not take him down in a 1to 1 battle. He looked left, there was a little handle of a bicycle, he thought about grabbing it and impaling it in the monster. But 1- if the monsters reflexes were good,(they would be) he would be annihilated before he even said: "My bad, this impaling thing was a small joke." 2-even if he could strike the monster, He doubted if the pointed handle would do any good against the hide of the beast. The hide looked like it was made of chromium. But then, his eyes fell on something in the partially broken museum, a sword. It was surrounded by a glass box, the sword had a silver hilt, with a blue gem situated in the handle. The blade was also silver, sparkling in the sun… he didn't know why. But he felt like he should go and pick up the sword. Ignoring the comments spiralling in his head, he quietly picked up the bicycle handle. And tucked it behind his shirt, he followed the monster till he reached the sword. And then quickly smashed the bicycle handle on the glass box, thankfully it broke or else it would have looked quite weird, he hit the box multiple times and the box not breaking. He pulled the sword, as soon as he held the sword, he felt a tinge of electricity vibrating every cell, every particle in his body, energy flowed into him. He looked at the goat, the goat yelled "Oh you wanna go the hard way, then bring it on." Blake did not know what happened to him energy burst in him, and he erupted in blue light. He did not know how he did it, but he leapt into the sky with his sword, and with incredible speed and power he brought down his sword on the monster, blue light splashed everywhere, and in a colossal blast he was gone, with the other half of the museum and trees which surrounded them. He just looked at the ground, where the monster had been had turned into dust, he looked around himself, the whole place had been turned into what looked like a crater, "Oh my!" said Blake, "I'm in serious trouble now." with that he collapsed, and stared into the blue sky where he saw a golden horse coming to him, his eyes slowly closed and then, he blacked out.

Chapter 3

He got up with a start, he blinked several times to see if he was dreaming, a nurse with green hair approached him. He looked around and saw he was lying on a comfy bed, with an object beside him. It was the sword, with which he impaled the goat, "No... No....No!" he screamed and got up from his bed, the nurse rushed to calm him down, but he just took off screaming. "It was real, it was real, that was not a dream!" He ran from the medical wing, the place which he was in looked like a kind of summer camp. Where there were different houses and a big amphitheatre or assembly area. There were several ponds to the right of the medical house, and there was a luscious green forest outside the camp. He also saw a river next to a kind of garden which ran along the river. There was also a steel gate, which was probably the entry gate. He forgot all about his dream, and just stared around, admiring the incredible beauty of the campsite, when somebody tapped his shoulders. He spun around and saw a man with a silver moustache, and a mean face. His stare was harsh and intense, with lightning blue eyes. Blake's first impression of the man was that he was too cold, he looked so cold that it looked like he used to live in some ice mountain in the middle of no-where.

"Excuse me, can you tell me what are you doing here?" Blake looked dumbfounded. Then the nurse came and explained "oh he is new here…" said the nurse. "What do u mean new?" Replied Blake, the nurse just smiled at him. "Master Domo will explain everything to you." said the nurse, looking at the moustache man, he just looked at Blake. "But before that we need to know who you are." "Well I'm Blake walker." "No, no!" smiled the moustache man, "I mean what is your hidden power!"

Blake was a little bit confused. Lately, he battled a Goat monster, vanished him with a magical sword and then ends up in this small camp with huts. Which was apparently for people with extreme power. Like shooting fireballs and stuff like that. As far as Blake knew, he did not have any great superpower, except for chugging 2bottles of coke at once. Now if that was considered a superpower, then Blake wondered the future and security of earth… Blake really was confused at this point. He thought Master Domo was gonna make them write a test paper or something. But of course, the newcomers needed to fight other experienced fighters in combat… Blake was taken into one of the houses to get ready for battle. A boy named Andrews, who was about 15-16 years, was dressing him for the fight. He made him wear a kind of black colour suit, for inners and outside, he wore a silver-plated chest armour with, leg paddings and hand paddings. Then he gave him his sword, the silver hilt gleamed in the moonlight, "Here you go, and best of luck." Blake thanked him, and asked "Hey, is the fight to death, or is there like a time limit?" Actually, there is no time limit. And we only do this so that the superpower of that person can be revealed, like if ur a magician, Then you might suddenly cast a spell on ur opponent with ought actually knowing what you are doing. And as for dying, the chances are pretty slim, because here we heal through magic, so our healing is better than the natural world." said Andrews. "But you are not the normal world, right?" "Yeah, I mean we belong in another dimension only, but that is not important, you rather get ready for your fight, cause you don't want to die." Said Andrews "But you said you couldn't die?" "I said the chances are pretty slim, but it has happened once.....it may happen again."

Andrews knew how to give a motivational talk, After telling Blake, there was a possibility of dying. Blake listened to all the instruction of the combat carefully and also did a few warm-ups just in case. "Mr Blake, please head up on stage right now." Blake headed up on stage, the stage was made of chromium the same substance his armour was made of. The stage was circular, big enough for a basketball court, with people surrounding it, there was a referee in the middle, building a wall between him and his opponent. He saw his opponent who was quite tall, but Andrews had assured him, he was of his age. Which meant he was 13-year-old.

The weapons she was carrying was a sword and a shield the same arms he was carrying. The referee yelled "Start the fight now!" and the match has begun. Blake was really nervous, he had never wielded a sword and shield before. But he surprisingly was good at it, he dodged most of his opponents strike, and also attacked him with his strikes as well, it was going good until Blake messed up. He started imagining a face forming on the opponents, shield, it was no other than, the very own goat monster. The image began to speak to him, his body went on autopilot. He began to understand why the goat was here, to distract him, but as much as he needed you get back In the fight. He wanted to hear what the goat was saying it whispered "I am not dead, I will come back and take my revenge on you." And then the goat smiled, and his vision broke away, distracting him, and then his opponent hit him with the shield on his chest and sent him flying to corner of the stadium. His ribs hurt, and his vision started to get blurred, his breath was gradually decreasing. He looked around the stadium, everyone was laughing and urging his opponent to finish him off. He looked at his opponent, he had a thin smirk on his face and said, "Let's finish this off then." And he raised his sword to finish Blake.

Blake thought this is over, but a voice inside him kept saying, "You can do it, you have the power of the dragon." and he looked at Master Domo, their eyes locked for a second. He looked at Blake with his cold blue stormy, eyes. And then, he nodded his head as if sending the same message. As soon as the point of the sword came crashing down at him, he dodged, and he got up, with a grin spread across my face. "Oh you got some dodging skills kid." said the opponent, "Oh, I got some other, skills in store for you too," said Blake, and he concentrated all his power, and closed his eyes, he started to remember. The blast of blue light he had summoned in the camping trip. He felt as if all the molecules in his body were vibrating as if they posses infinite energy and they wanted to break loose. He felt as if he was superheating, letting drop all the grudge he had. He opened his eyes and saw the aghast look his opponent was wearing. And then he came to know why he looked at himself, and he was glowing a majestic blue aura. He then looked at his opponent and spread his arms. The huge aura which was surrounding him, spread across the stadium, causing a massive explosion which ripped the stadium and toppled several trees. Blake, looked around, campers were scrambling everywhere, but Master Domo and several other heads just had a horrified expression on their face, and they looked at one another. Blake couldn't think anything at this point, he just heard campers screaming, and the safety guard shouting at everyone to go inside. He collapsed, his eyelids, slowly collapsing and the noise, gradually, drowned, and then Blake passed out.

Blake woke up, at the medical wing of the camp, like he had just bench pressed 200 pounds, with burning tinfoil in his mouth. But soon Master Domo came around and explained what happened to him yesterday. Blake realised he had done worse. He quickly got dressed, and went out for breakfast, but before that he gargled 5 times with water because getting rid of the taste of burning foil can be tough. He went outside and sat at the table of newcomers, but he found it a bit strange that all the campers avoided eye contact with him, and as soon as he sat at the newcomers' table, five people just left the table and joined some other table. He mostly guessed it was because of the duel yesterday. For about 10-15 minutes, he just quietly ate his toast with jam and some chocolate milk. But then he heard some people across the table snickering and looking at him. This time, he didn't lose eye contact, so one guy at that table just smirked and looked at him.

Chapter 4

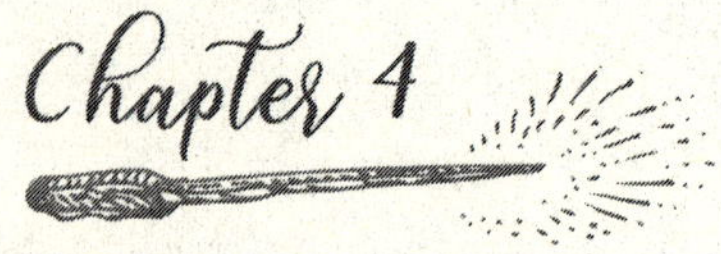

The guy got up and approached him, "Hey, kid up and get outta here, you don't deserve to be here." He had wavy black hair, a healthy well built body like a pro athlete, and had a deep resonating voice. Blake just remained fixed in his chair. "Hey, you don't understand kid, nobody messes with Crasher here." "Cool nickname," said Blake, sarcastically. Crasher just looked into Blake's eyes coldly, he simply grabbed Blake by his collar lifted him up and punched Blake in the stomach, Blake fell onto the ground groaning, with drops of blood sprouting from his mouth. "See, I told you! You don't belong here." Blake spontaneously became. Still, he felt as if a sudden rush of energy was filling him up, charging every molecule, every particle in his body, his senses magnified, suddenly he could see everything in great detail, he could also see the flow of energy oozing out of objects, his hands felt like live cannons waiting to fire, and then he burst into electrifying blue light.

He only remembered bits and pieces which was the same because he would have enjoyed seeing "crasher" crashing into two tables in a great blast. He climbed out of the bed of the medical wing. For the third time since he arrived at the camp, and this was a streak, Blake wasn't proud of. He went to the wing of masters. Where he thought Master Domo would be, but when he went to ask the secretary there, she said he had gone for a meeting. Blake had a tiny suspicion that the meeting was regarding Blake. He said thank you to secretary and headed out to the billboard where the daily events were listed out. The big event listed out for today was called the "golden horse" where apparently you were put in a team. And your team needed to find a statue of a horse by certain clue given to you, while you were doing this you also needed to battle out opponents to reach the horse first. Whoever found the golden horse first, won the game. The game sounded pretty interesting to Blake because he always liked treasure hunting when he was small. But the rules of treasure hunting here were placed a little different from those of earth because apparently you did not need to kill your opponent just to get to the treasure first. The term opponent reminded Blake of the incident which happened just recently. While he was eating breakfast, so he decided in courtesy to go check on the so called "Crasher" Blake didn't know that another person was waiting for him, to take him somewhere, and that person would not take no for an answer.

Blake saw Master Domo sauntering through the strawberry fields. Blake wondered why he was calling him. He thought that it was because of crasher, but clearly master had something else to say he had a tense look on his face and soon scowled when he saw Blake approaching. Blake took that as a negative sign. Master Domo looked at Blake and said- "I realised who you are and what you came here for." Blake replied, "I am Blake, and I was put in this camp, you know this." Domo replied "Not that, let me show you." And with a snap of his fingers the world dissolved.

Chapter 5

Blake woke up riding a horse, which was pretty strange, considering that he had no memory of how he got there. Master Domo was riding beside him soaring through the clouds on a magical and majestic horse which could fly as fast as a bolt of lightning. Master Domo pointed downwards towards the ground for Blake to see. Blake got up groggily, and looked down, he was astonished by what he saw. Valleys were filled with fluffy cloud like ice, there were humongous and gigantic snow capped mountains sprawling everywhere. And inside those valleys was a sublime and enormous castle with a looming tower reaching the skies. "What's that?" Blake asked, "well, that is the ice-palace" replied Master Domo. "That is where the ice world gets its power from," said Master Domo while pointing to a blinding blue light coming from the sky and entering the tower. "No one can harness that much power with ought wielding the Infinity Blade first, And only the king of the ice world has the authority to wield it." said Master Domo " Can it be stolen?" said Blake, "It has once been stolen and it can happen again but the chance of that happening is quite slim. But I believe it is about to be stolen and if it has to be stolen. It would be terrible for us because as soon as a powerful object like that gets stolen the energy balance is shifted and the world falls under the dark dimension." said Master Domo "Whats the dark dimension?" Asked Blake "The dark dimension is a dimension where all the worlds fall into when they lose their power source." Replied Master Domo "does the dark dimension have a ruler ?" Asked Blake "Well we are not sure, but last time one of ours betrayed us and waged a battle against us to take all the dimensions under control. But a saviour and his group of teammates defeated the ruler in an epic battle which shook all the dimensions, in the end the saviour and his group of teammates won the battle. And the saviour returned the original power sources to their places, but one power source was remaining, it was the power- source which held his life form together. But if he wanted peace in all dimensions again he had to return the power- source. Which he got in his rightful place, therefore he sacrificed his life to maintain order and peace in the world, but before he went. He said that whenever the ruler of the dark dimension would return, his power would be given to someone worthwhile. And a team of five would fight the forces of evil. Hence this prophecy was started, we knew the prophecy would come, we just didn't know when." said Master Domo, "This story is nice, and all, but could have not told this to me in the camp instead. You brought me here in a horse flying in the sky above the ice- world, it is so cold!!" Master Domo said "I did not want any one to listen to this conversion." The colour from Blake's face slowly drained out, making him look like ghost. "So....so..I am....I am one of the sa.....Saiviours? " Blake stammered, Master Domo just gave the kind of sarcastic smile the teacher gives before telling you that you have failed and that she would be calling your parents. "Now let me guess, I need to go on a quest to find one of the power sources and find a way to keep it safe?" said Blake "No, you need to find a stone which provided access to the dimension where one of the crystal is kept. And then you need to bring it here to the camp, and not only that. The servants of the Emperor would also be there to get the crystal before you get it. So you will be on a race to find the power source first. But before that you need to find out where it is, and just warning you. They are going to track you and try to kill you as soon as you step out of the camp. So you also need to be on constant watch. And you can only take 2 more campers for the quest because others need to be there to defend the camp. So are you ready?" Blake looked aghast as if he just got a call from death saying that he will come and pick Blake up tomorrow, "Oh wait! He did". Blake said "I wish I wouldn't have gone for that stupid picnic and stayed home and none of this would have happened." Master Domo smiled enthusiastically and said "Best of luck, you will need it, and you were meant to be here Blake. Such a catastrophic event has not happened in a thousand years. Where all the dimensions start collapsing and their entrances open." Blake looked could not decide whether to kill himself or this stupid white haired master. He decided on the first one, so he said, "Fine I will go get that stupid power source, and I will be back by supper."

Blake was having a terrible day, first Master Domo tricked him into going into a trip. And instead of making him visit places and introducing him to new areas and making him meet people. He took him to that "Ice-kingdom." and freaked him out of his mind about that ruler who anted to take over the world and stuff. Not only that. The Master's way of welcoming him into the camp included him handing over a stupid quest. About a lost crystal which would save the world or something like that. And this quest wasn't the typical treasure hunt you play at birthday parties. This type of journey meant reaching the treasure first with a bunch of ninja assassins. Tailing you and waiting for that moment to obliterate you from existence as soon as you catch you forty winks or use the bathroom or something. With that, the master also narrated a fairy tale story about a "Saviour." And how is power would be descended to a worthy person as soon as the Emperor woke up from his century old afternoon nap? And Blake seemed to have just the rotten luck to get that power. He didn't want to be a saviour or a hero or anything like that. He just wanted to be a regular guy with a normal lifestyle which did not include a bunch of assassin goats. With a lousy accent trying to kill him with their fashionable wardrobe. But alas, destiny had other plans for him.

Chapter 6

The day burned so quickly that Blake didn't know that it was time for dinner. Until his stomach screamed in protest. He sat down at the newcomers, from the corner of his eyes, he saw crasher. (Looking like a mummy wrapped in bandages) Staring at him, as soon as he turns his head in his direction. Crasher looked away. Clearly, he was not going to mess with him again. This time no one gave him dirty looks at the table or moved away when he sat. Blake had a strong feeling that the campers either so he goes with Master Domo. Or they knew about the conversion he had with Master Domo. So they thought he was really important in this camp or something. While he was eating dinner, an announcement was made about his quest. And that he was supposed to chose 2 more people for they quest, an that he will be announcing the names today night. Blake froze, he hadn't given a thought about who he was going to chose yet. And he didn't want to make a fool out of himself in front of everyone. Everyone slowly shuffled to the podium, and Blake climbed up on the stage next to the fighting arena. Master Domo was waiting for him, he smiled at Blake and then looked at the campers, he began "Good evening, today I'm here to announce a new quest, which our newcomer Blake Miller, will be completing, I know you all may have some doubts as to why he is chosen for this quest even though he is a newcomer. Well today I'm here to clear those doubts. I'm here to announce that Blake is one of the saviours, and yes, the dark Emperor is awakening."

The audiences faces froze, it was like that somebody had just announced the end of the world, well technically it had been announced. Blake did not understand why he thought if their saviour was announced then they should be happy. But then it struck Blake like a bolt of lightning that why even the council people. And Master Domo had a frightened expression on their face. Because if he is the saviour then the other part of the prophecy would also be true which is that the Emperor is awakening. And that there would be a 60-40 chance that Blake would win this war. That is why the campers and the council members did not want this prophecy to happen because if it did. Then they were more likely to lose. That is why they were so freaked out. Blake was so lost in his thoughts that he didn't pay attention to Master Domo calling his name, "Now Blake will say the names of the people who he wants to choose for his quest...... Blake?" "Yes...Yes." Blake stammered, he did not know what to say "The people I want to choose for my quest are....Ummm they are..." Blake was trembling with fear. Everyone gave him nasty looks, then out of the blue, one girl raised her hand and shouted "He chose Oscar and me." Blake looked dumbfounded, he just mindlessly nodded his head. "Very well, Blake has chosen Amber and Oscar for his quest, they may proceed of the quest after a month of training and planning. "Thank you for being with us today." Said Master Domo, Blake looked like he had just committed the biggest blunder of his life. Instead of carefully analysing each campers strength an powers. Thinking of the best possible way how each camper would add to the success of the mission. And being incisive about whom to chose and whom not to, Blake just took a shot in the dark and chose two random campers. Who he did not know, to go and save the world from a multiverse crises which threatened the existence of every being in the universe. Wow, the day was looking good…So he just went to his assigned bunk and crashed there for the night.

Chapter 1

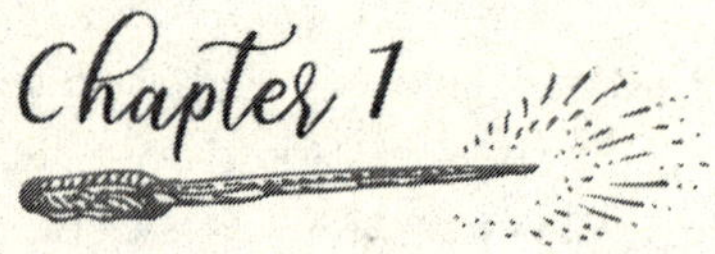

He woke up feeling somewhat rejuvenated, he washed up in about half-an hour and headed over for breakfast. He ate breakfast in about 15 mins his standard breakfast was fried eggs, bread and jam and some chicken sausages. His schedule for his team and him for today was working on their magical powers, sword fighting, and practising war.

He headed over for the sword fighting class. He had no past experience in sword fighting. But he knew he would be good at it because he had a monster with a sword once. He suddenly remembered where his sword was, he quickly ran to the inventory item house next to the medical wing. And found a box named Blake inscribed on the top. He opened it and found his sword inside, he held it in his hand, it had the perfect weight balance. Not to heavy to hold not to light, it was like this sword was made for his hand. He scrutinized the sword, it was silver with blue stripes on the hilt. There was a spherical mark on the hilt, It might be for a gem or something Blake thought. He quickly closed the box and sprinted towards the sword fighting arena. There were only three more people in the sword fighting arena, amber and Oscar and the teacher, “Hello! I’m ur teacher who will train you in sword fighting, my name is Noah.” He smiled at all three of them, he had warm orange eyes, with hair neatly trimmed. He had a well built body and was about 5’8. They all bowed in front of him, “Oh! Blake I see you have got a sword of your own.” “Yes, master I have.” Blake said, “Now all of you go get dressed into your safety armour.” said Master Noah. After Blake was done dressing into his armour he went over to Amber and Oscar. The armour was surprisingly light but durable. Then he remembered that the armour was crafted through magic and chromium. He went to amber and said “Hi!. Um thanks for volunteering for the quest. I was really lost about whom to pick then.” Amber had pink hair with pink eyes, a rare combination. “That’s ok, I volunteered cause I really wanted to go for a quest.”

Said amber with a half-hearted smile. “Same,” said Oscar, Oscar had deep sea green eyes, with blonde hair. He held out his hand to Blake and said “Welcome to the team.” Blake shook hands with Oscar and almost got a fracture, “Heck of a grip man.” Said Blake rubbing his fingers. Oscar just gave a mischievous smile, “All right kiddos its time to fight.” Said Master Noah, “You ready? Cause this is your first time fighting, and this is like our 15th time.” Said Oscar, “Oh sword fighting is a piece of cake.” Blake said while trying to muster up a confident smile.

Blake got knocked down flat on the face for the 15th time since he started practice. In his defence Amber and Oscar were using their powers to beat him, and he was not using his powers. Cause well… He didn't know how to after the 16th time amber knocked Blake down with her powers Blake had enough. But still Blake was stupefied with their powers. Amber could pull out a card, and that card would do some kind of magic, like fire a concentrated high energy beam. Which glowed pink or she would open a portal, go inside it and come out from another one which spawned randomly across the arena, which also glowed pink. Oscar was the same height as Blake but was much more athletic and agile than Blake, his power was to burn with the energy of a supernova. Which was really handy, when it came to battle. Oscar told him that he got more energy around a power source like dynamite. Which was exploding or something like that, and Ambers powers grew around stuff like energy beams or electricity. Or anything which supplied a constant source of electricity. And Blake well he didn't know how to use his superpower. Master Noah called for a break, Blake approached the master and said "I want to know how I can use my superpower, please tell me" Master Noah smiled and said, "Ok step into the arena." Blake did as he was told, "Now stand still and close your eyes, picture something which you like, and that gives you immense joy." Blake pictured a waterfall, and a mountainside in which cool breeze was touching his face. "Now channel the energy you find in that image into yourself." Blake started imagining that the energy he was experiencing was coming in his hand slowly. Increasing like a bolt of deadly thunder waiting to strike. He felt his palms grow hot and he felt the same thing which he felt when he battled that goat, As if every molecule, every atom in his body was supercharging waiting to expel enormous amounts of energy. He opened his eyes, what he saw was astonishing. Blue mist curled around him, and occasionally strikes of bright blue energy would collide with the ground forming the blue mist. He concentrated on his hand, and a spherical bright blue shape started forming in his hand. "Now try to shoot it!" Yelled Master Noah and Blake shot his spherical object. A bright beam of energy shot across the room hitting the door, but thankfully the door was made of chromium. So it didn't erupt, but the impact was so powerful it knocked the cupboard of armour. Bursting it in a million pieces. Blake was astonished, but as soon as he went to admire his work but he collapsed because of the sheer exhaustion.

He woke up about 20 mins later in the sword fighting arena, Master Noah just smiled at him and said "That was truly spectacular, you mastered your power in just one try only. And harnessing that type of power in such a short period of time is nothing less than marvellous. Practise your power just a few ew more times and you won't faint." Blake just smiled and nodded his head, he was really satisfied that he now won't need to go to battle undefended. And Amber and Oscar wont need to be behind his back all the time protecting him, now he could protect himself.

He was sitting with Amber and Oscar, for lunch, and he was trying not to look at crasher. But he just could not avoid it, as soon as he looked at him. He realised Crasher was also looking at him. Frightened Crasher turned his head and started looking in the opposite direction "The event scheduled for next week is called find the magical horse said amber you know that that is right?" Said Amber. Blake said "Yeah you need to find a statue of a golden horse before the other teams do, with certain clues. And you can attack other teams if they get to the flag first." "And one more thing, you are allowed to use your magical powers in this event. Which would put us in a great advantage, because you know, you have a special set of powers. And you would be at a greater competitive advantage over the rest." Blake just shook his head as if he had thought about this before and planned all the tactics. The truth was Blake did not even know that this event was being held today, and about the whole. "Competitive advantage." Blake knew it wasn't true because he could just use his power once before collapsing for about 45 mins. So instead of being an asset to the team, he would become a liability. But he couldn't let that happen he couldn't let his team down. They were so kind and accepting. And Amber had saved him for the embarrassment when choosing his team. He couldn't just let them down now after they did so much for him. "Don't worry, we're gonna win that magical horse," said Blake with a determined smile.

Chapter 8

The next 7 days, burnt so fast that Blake did not even realise it that today was the day The magical horse event was being held. He had trained so hard that he hadn't realised that a week was over at the camp. Every day he went to the sword fighting arena. Worked on his magical powers and trained continuously for 4 hours with Master Noah on his sword fighting skills. After so much training he had started to feel that the sword was guiding him to his target. And he could hit any target with ought looking. He even stood firm against Ambers portal attack, because somehow his sword targeted him to his target. Master Noah said this was because his energy and the swords energy were now in sync. That is why he could feel other energy sources around him. He was all ready for the event tonight, he quickly got dressed and went to eat breakfast. He met Amber and Oscar at the table. Oscar enthusiastically told them about the plans he made for tonight's big event. Amber and Blake made corrections to his plans. When breakfast had finished the three had made a foolproof plan that they hoped to achieve. They gave a high-five to each other and

Blake had never felt so happy in his life, and this was one moment Blake would never forget.

He started to get dressed up in his armour. Today was the big event where he could prove himself worthy. He got out of the dressing tent, it was kind of chilly, Blake headed towards the starting line of the event. He remembered all the battle plans. And was ready to go, he met Amber and Oscar at the starting line in the forest. The forest was dark and gloomy, with many swamps inside it, But Master Domo had assured everyone the forest was secured, and no monster was lurking inside the forest. He explained that the forest was a part of the camp and that the camp was surround by a magical barrier, with towers of archer. Sprawling across the border, so unauthorised entering of the camp was near to impossible. But some part of Blake said that the border could be passed. And that's what scared Blake the most. Because he just felt some tingling feeling, that someone was watching him and something unpleasant was about to happen. Ignoring the feeling, he got ready, Master Domo shouted "All right people, get ready,1… 2… 3 and go!" Blake stayed put in his place. He looked at amber and nodded. Amber took out a card, pink light was scattered everywhere and they dissapered into that light.

Blake couldn't feel anything, he just felt that he was falling and after about 5 seconds he found himself lying in the grass. He looked around, Oscar and amber were next to him, he got up and looked, they were on top of a hill. This was their plan, they would chose high ground so that no camper would be able to attack them. They looked around, and suddenly a symbol blazed in front of them, it was like a hologram. Which was translucent, the image on the hologram was a picture of a castle. Which Blake new of because he could just see the castle about 2 hills away. The hologram shut down, He looked at amber and said "Can you teleport us over there?" "I can only teleport us to the next hill, after that they will block all teleportations." said Amber "Ok then do that." In a couple of seconds they were on the next hill, they started to walk down. And then amber froze in her tracks. She whispered Oscar and Blake to look down and then Blake saw a group of other campers. They couldn't see them, but it would be not long before they spotted them. One was carrying a bow, the other one was carrying a spear. The third one was carrying a sword, Blake whispered "Let's go and attack them now, we will have the element of surprise, and we can take them down because two of them have far ranged weapons. Which won't do any good in a hand to hand combat. The third one has a sword. Which might be a problem but we can handle that because. As soon as we finish taking on the two it will be a 3 vs 1 match. Amber you go on the one with the bow, Oscar you go on the one with the spear. And ill go on the guy with the sword." Both of them nodded in agreement. Blake concerted hard, after about a second swirly blue mists started coming out of him. He took out his sword jumped and said "Surprise fellas." He gave a straight cut on the sword guys shoulder. The girl with the bow and arrow called out "Andrew look out!" But it was too late, Andrew had crumbled to the ground. Thankfully Andrew was wearing armour or else he would have been obliterated. The girl with the bow nocked an arrow, but Amber threw a card at her bow, and the bow exploded in pink light. The bow went flying, and so did the girl, He then saw Oscar batting the girl with the spear. The girl threw the spear at Oscar, but Oscar held out his hand, and a beam of golden light hit the spear, and the spear disintegrated. Blake was so distracted that he didn't notice Andrews grabbing his sword. Andrews lunged, and with one deadly strike he hit Blake on his back. Blake felt pain shoot up in his spine, and then Blake collapsed. His vision became blurry, and eyes stared dimming. Deep down Blake new he wasn't dying, but the pain was so much that it left him paralysed. Then he remembered that he had promised his friends Amber and Oscar that they would win this. He turned and saw Amber fight of the girl with the bow. She kept screaming for Blake to get up, but he just couldn't, and then he remembered. The intense struggle he did for this very day, and then he slowly and steadily got up. Andrews had a grin on his face and said "So this is our saviour, right here who cant fend off one attack, how will he save the universe from the threat that is coming?" Andrew gave a sly smile and said, "Come on show what you got Blake, or are you just an imposter?" Blake got up gave a grin and said "Oh you want to see what I can do? I'll show you." Blake concentrated all his energy in his palms. A sphere of glowing blue light emerged he gave a grin and said "This is what I can do" he threw the energy sphere on Andrews. And a big explosion knocked a tree, and Andrews went flying, and he landed with a groan. The girl with the bow got so startled that she turned. And Amber saw this as her chance to attack she threw a card and this time a pink circle on the ground around. The girl appeared, the girl looked down, and then the circle burst into pink smoke. The girl came out of the smoke choking and gasping then she collapsed. At the same time Oscar shot a wave of golden light which wrapped the girl with the spear. The girl started glowing and in moments, she became normal. But all her armour had melted, and then even she collapsed. The three looked at each other nodded and moved forward. Three eagles came, and they took the three unconscious hopefully campers to the medical wing. This made Blake feel a bit uneasy because this meant that the council was monitoring each and every move they made. They headed into the swamp. It was cold and dark, this place was rather risky because they had no cover and they would be easily spotted because now each one of them was glowing like their respective powers. Blake was glowing blue, Oscar was glowing golden, and Amber was glowing a shade of pink and red. As they were moving, they heard a sound in the swamp. All of them immediately stopped in their tracks. Blake looked around he couldn't spot anyone. He tried to remember the class he had for sporting the direction of the sound. He focused hard, and he came to know where the sound was coming from. It was coming from behind the hill just next to the swamp. He peered in that direction and saw two shuffling feet behind a boulder next to the hill. Blake pointed the location to Amber and Oscar, Blake said "Let's attack them now, they won't be ready for the attack, and that way we have more chances of winning." Amber and Oscar nodded, they quietly inched forward. Amber pulled out a card and threw it at the edge of the boulder. The card exploded in pink smoke, and the people who were behind the boulder emerged coughing, and then they collapsed. Amber and Oscar inched forward towards the two campers. But Blake didn't feel right, he thought why were there only two campers? And where was the third one? Suddenly realisation struck him, he yelled to Amber and Oscar "Get away from them now! It's a trap!" Amber looked at him with an uneasy frown, and said "What?" Blake ran towards her and said "Those two campers are being kept hostages, the third one has been taken to the medical wing. This is a trap, that is why they got injured so quickly because they were already injured. This is a big trap, we need to leave immediately" Ambers was horrified. She looked at Blake and then at Oscar, the two shouted in unison- "Oscar come here now!" Oscar looked at them, and just frowned, he started approaching them. He opened his mouth to say something, but he could not complete it, because a silver arrow went past Blake. And hit the ground in front of Oscar. About a millisecond past and then the arrow burst, sending Blake and Amber flying through the air. Blake hit hard on a rock Amber fell in the swamp. Blake tried to get up despite his head spinning and his nose overflowing with blood. Blake said to himself "Well I guess this is just a payback of what I did to Alex."

And got up, his sword solidified in his hand, smashing blue mist. Amber got up with disks glowing bright red, and several geometric shapes are drawn on it. Another arrow came flying at them, but this time they were ready. Amber threw one of the discs at the arrow and the disk sort of absorbed the explosion. A camper jumped from a tree behind Blake, with a sword. But Blake defended the strike and punched the camper in the stomach. The camper stumbled behind, and Blake gave a strike on his back with his sword. The camper yelped and collapsed, the cut on his armour glowing a bright shade of red. Blake was fascinated with what his sword could do? If he had just put a bit of more power. The whole campers armour would have been shattered and would have melted in a puddle of armour goo. Blake looked at the camper puffed. Blake turned around and saw Amber was fighting another camper. She was doing well then he turned to see Oscar. And felt guilt rising up his throat, he had completely forgotten about Oscar. The arrow had just been a stone's throw away from him if Blake's nose was bleeding so terribly and he was feeling dizzy. Then he tried to imagine what would happen to Oscar. He quickly hurried to find Oscar, in the swamp screaming "Oscar! Oscar!" He felt so terrible, he thought what if he had just lost his friend. And then he heard a familiar voice that kind of voice you hear at circuses or a party or something. The kind of voice which is buzzing with excitement and energy like a little kid. "Hey man Blake, why are looking so depressed?" asked Oscar. Blake smiled and hugged Oscar, and said- "How is this possible you aren't even injured one bit." Oscar said "I think my body kind of absorbed that energy because that is also kind of my power. If I am exposed to high sources of energy like a blast or something my body absorbs that energy." Blake now for the first time felt kind of dissatisfied with his power, but nevertheless he was happy that his friend was alive. "Ok guys are you like done with whole emotional part because I'm kind of bored right here." Amber yelled "Look back!" Before Blake could locate the source of the anonymous sound he felt a blow on his chest. The force of the blow was so powerful that it knocked him flat on the ground.

Chapter 9

He scrambled near a Huge boulder for cover, he was scared and shocked at the moment, not the best emotions to fight with. He analysed his wound. It was not a major wound because most of the shock had been absorbed by the armour. He had been hit by a powerful sword that is why part of his arm was injured. He peeked from behind the boulder, Oscar and Amber were already on the person. It looked like they knew this camper because they were calling him Jacob. He looked about 2 to 3 years older than Blake and had obviously more experience because he could fend of Oscar and Ambers attack single handedly. While joking about trash puns which most likely he made. something like this "Hey Oscar if I slash your left side out, would you be all right?" Blake tried to think of Jacobs weakness. Jacobs currently biggest weakness was that he had forgotten. That Blake was hiding behind the boulder because he was so caught up in his stupid puns and fighting Oscar and Amber.

Blake thought if he could surprise Jacob by firing a beam of energy. Then Jacob would be distracted by trying to dodge the beam of energy and while he was doing that Amber and Oscar could attack him. Jacobs team had already been injured because he was not a team player and was overconfident, it was time to use that against him. Blake concentrated hard his palms felt hot, and then a sphere of crinkling blue energy materialised in his hand. He focused more, and the bright blue wisps started increasing, and that's when he heard someone shout "Blake help!" And he made the biggest mistake. Which he could possibly do he turned around to see what the commotion was and saw a girl smiling at him. Blake then partially remembered a lecture from the superpowers identification class. The teacher had explained that one of the powers people had was to manipulate emotions and voice that was what the girl had done. Blake didn't have time to react, the girl pierced a dagger in his shoulder armour, it didn't completely pierce the armour. But the impact still hurt Blake, he clenched his arm, and an expression of horror started to show on Blake's face when he saw green light spilling from his shoulder plate. The girl said "Oh, I think I forgot to tell you that after I impale my enemies. My power is focused on my dagger, and it explodes." she gave a cynical smile. As soon as she did that Blake burst into green light, he found himself lying on the ground. Dust was flying everywhere, he slowly took support of the rock (or whatever was left out of it and) and very got up. He looked over the boulder Blake, and Oscar was lying on the ground, unconscious. He looked at that Girl she smiled and waved to Jacob, Blake was so foolish to think that only Jacob was left in his team. The girl was in Jacobs team Blake focused hard on his palms, and then the girl interrupted and said "Oh that won't work now because you have used most of your energy in random bursts of energy. Unlike us you have still not learnt how to control your energy Flow and save some for later." Blake looked at the girl with his mouth wide open, he had used up all his energy. And now they were going to get defeated, now there was no one to save them. Amber and Oscar were both unconscious, he had not concentrated on his energy flow, and now he was doomed. He sat down on the ground sobbing. His dream and his team's dream had now been completely destroyed because of his carelessness. But now an idea struck his brain like lightning. He looked up at the girl and said "You said that I have almost finished my power, right?" "Yeah why?" said the girl, Blake looked around he saw the sacred rock where the great dagger was found by the founder of the camp. It had to be atlas 1000 years old. Master Domo had shown the newcomers this spot in one of his classes. Blake looked around. He thought if he sprinted there he could reach thee in about 2 minutes. It was a crazy idea, but it was worth a shot. He smiled deliriously at Jacob. He now felt a surge of hope. He still hadn't been defeated he could still win the magical horse. So he got up brushed his pants said "See you later folks." And ran at full speed towards the sacred rock, leaving Amber and Oscar at the hands of Jacob and the girl.

Blake really didn't know what he was doing. Dashing into the woods was the last thing Jacob and the girl had expected. It would have left them stunned and bought them a few precious seconds. It was a stupid idea, but it was the only chance he got against the duo. He had exhausted his supply of magical powers because he was not trained to conserve it, and his two teammates were injured. The odds were really very bad. Blake knew he couldn't fight the duo because they were overpowered and he didn't have any magical power left. He jumped over a rock and continued to run, he looked back, sure enough, Jacob and the girl were following him. He expected them to follow him because they couldn't just leave him like that, they wanted the point for elimination. Blake saw again, just a quick glance, the girl was knocking an arrow. He didn't know she had a bow, it was risky now because she was a trained professional and would have obviously learnt to shoot moving targets. The best chance of her not shooting him was to change his track multiple numbers of times and run in random directions. He did that, and after a couple of seconds, a blazing orange coloured arrow streaked past him. That was really close. He continued to run and was just about to reach the rock, in about 20 seconds. He glanced back she was knocking another arrow, this would be her last shot, 15 seconds almost there. He was just about to reach the rock when he heard a whizz. Which was the sound of the fatal projectile tearing through the air? He was just about to reach when he felt a burning sensation on his shoulder. The pain was so intense that he immediately stopped, dropped on the ground and clutched his scorching arm in immense pain. He heard the sound of two pairs of approaching feet. He tried to get up, but black spots danced across his eyes, just a couple of seconds and the duo would be here. Eliminating him and his teammates from the game, or worse he would himself pass out from the pain, he looked at this arm. The projectile had grazed him, he was just a couple of meters away from the glowing purple rock, he started to crawl towards the rock. Every move made him wince in pain, but he had to do it. "Still trying to run away Blake." said Jacob, "It's futile now," said Jacob smirkingly, he was just about to touch it when he heard the girl knock an arrow. She was just about to fire when he touched the rock and yelled so loudly that his voice echoed from the rocks around. Nothing happened he looked at Jacob and the girl, he knew for sure that they thought he had officially lost it. A couple of more seconds were passed in awkward silence when the rock started glowing. Jacob and the girl had started to turn back to run, but they were too late. The rock glowed brighter and brighter and then it erupted into purple light.

Chapter 10

Blake was feeling pretty good of himself, he successfully wiped out a duo and regained his powers and healed himself. He headed over uphill to free Amber and Oscar. His plan had worked somehow, but what he didn't expect was another supplement package of full health and magical bonus powers. He had chosen the rock because, in his little tour, Master Domo had told him that this rock was a sacred spot where a mighty sword was kept decades ago. And, when he was doing some research in the library about the savior. It said that sometimes the magical powers are enhanced whenever you go near a sacred, powerful location or object that has been kept for more than hundreds of years. Blake just took a shot in the dark that this rock was sacred. But whatever the case, his plan worked. He headed over to Oscar and Amber. He opened up a bottle of flask which contained elixir, a type of magical drink only meant for people like them. The drink healed your body and provided comfort and relaxation. Amber and Oscar each drank about 3 sips of the elixir. Excess of the elixir could cause damage to your body because the different energies in your body started colliding with the elixir.

After they were done, Oscar and Amber got up to thank Blake, they hugged each other because of the near elimination experience they just had. After they were done they asked Blake how he fought against 2 heavily armed and experienced duo, because they were unconscious. Blake just shook his head and promised them that he would tell them about this some other time. Preferably for dinner after they win this competition and are announced winners in the grand hall with a feast. They headed over to the mountains, the castle was now a stone's throw away. They were about to go inside the castle from the main gate when Amber stopped them. " If we enter the castle from the main gate, it could be a trap because some teams might be expecting us to do that. They could be waiting for us ready to strike as soon as we're not paying attention." She said. Blake looked at Amber, she obviously had done quests like these many times. If it weren't for her, they would have gotten eliminated as soon as they would have entered the gate. "Let's enter the castle from the top, we can climb the hill adjacent to it and jump on it from above," said Oscar. Blake and Amber nodded their head. They started climbing the hill, in about 10 minutes they were on the peak overlooking the castle, they went to the edge and ducked. It was a risky jump if they managed they would reach the top floor of the castle. As they were just about to jump another sign blazed in front of them. It was a layout of the castle.

The castle contained six different floors each with a balcony. But the third floor glowed a bit brighter than the rest and was a shade of golden. "So the horse is hidden on the third floor!" Exclaimed Oscar. The hologram shut off they all went to the edge of the mountain. Currently they could see none of the other teams or an unexpected ambush. They looked at each other, clearly thinking how would they make the jump onto the terrace. Just then amber's palms started glowing red, and then suddenly she pulled out a rope which glowed bright red. She got up threw one end of the rope onto the terrace balcony, and it magically attached itself onto the railing. With that rope they could easily swing and land onto the 5th floor balcony. Skipping any traps or dangers on the terrace. Blake and Oscar looked at her and silently clapped. She just smirked at them. Amber was the first to jump, after that Oscar and then Blake.

Blake landed on the balcony of the fifth floor. He landed on his toes so that he would land quietly because stealth was the key in these kinds of situations. He slowly and quietly opened the door of the balcony and got inside. The floor was massive but dingy. All the corners of the floor were pitch dark. The wooden staircase was at the edge of the floor, looking gloomy and spooky. So basically this was your typical haunted house with a twist because this haunted house didn't have ghosts. This haunted house had even spookier thing lurking in the dark, it had a magical golden horse floating around somewhere with a bunch of people with magical powers trying to eliminate you.

Blake saw Amber and Oscar waiting for him in the corner. Their faces were also a shade of pale white. So Blake wasn't the only one scared here. Blake and Oscar followed amber down the spiral staircase which led them to the last floor. Amber ducked down and motioned them to follow. They crept alongside the staircase and waited for any sound to come, they waited for a while. Blake was just about to get up and climb down when he heard a faint crash. He peeked and saw a duo, just approaching them. He unsheathed his sword and got ready, any second now they would spot them. His hand became tense they were just about to approach, and then suddenly he heard two arrows whiz by him, slicing through the air. In about a millisecond both the duos were knocked down. He looked back, Ambers bow had already started to dissolve in pixels of bright pink. He looked at amber with shocked expression on his face. Amber just grinned at him. Blake used to think that he was one of the most powerful heroes, but now he knew he was wrong. The shot that Amber took was less than a millisecond that too with two arrows and with 100% accuracy. That was an impossible shot, but Amber took it and was successful. This kind of scared Blake, he wondered what would happen to him if he ever came on the wrong side of Amber. They followed Amber out of the floor onto the staircase, kind of by default. They were always behind her. Just one more floor to go, and then they would reach the floor which held the golden horse. As they were just going on to staircase, Blake heard Amber scream "Blake look out!" But Blake was too slow to react, as soon as he turned behind he felt a blow on his back. He collapsed and hit his head on the wall, Amber came to help him, but another camper hit her with his shield on her leg. She crumpled and grabbed her ankle, the injury must have been really intense because now Amber was screaming in pain. Two campers grabbed Oscar, one stabbed him in the leg. But Oscar's hand started glowing bright orange. He thrust both his arms forward, two bright beams energy knocked both campers. One flew out of the window, and one got hit on the wall next to staircase, and got plastered on the floor. Oscar then grabbed his leg. He winced a couple of times but finally managed to tie a scarf around his leg. Blake managed to get up, his head was bleeding, but it was minor. Ambers injury was major, her whole ankle was purple, and every time she was trying to take step, she was grimacing in pain. After all of them had tended their wounds. They were ready to go down, but then they heard shuffling feet, coming from the staircase. Amber looked at Blake she said "Blake, you need to go down and get the magical horse, because more campers would be coming from the staircase. And while we are fighting them, someone else might go down and claim the horse." Blake said "But icant just go down and leave you guys like this, both of you are seriously injured." Amber said "If you really care for us, go claim that horse and win this competition." Blake looked at Oscar, he nodded his head, for the first time in a while, he was serious. Oscar looked at Blake and said "Let's go and bust some heads" Blake smiled at Oscar, After a second of silence. The whole staircase erupted, and 2 squads came crashing down, fighting each other. "Amber yelled "Blake run!" Blake ran down the staircase, but what he didn't know was what awaited him.

Chapter 11

Blake was really tensed at this moment. His breathing was laboured, he felt really scared. He reached the doorway, he peeked inside, there was no one, but the whole place was illuminated by golden light. He double checked just in case someone was waiting behind the door, ready to attack him. As soon as he stepped inside, he also checked for traps or fatal ambushes. After he was done, he finally stepped inside, but he still felt something was lurking here. Just waiting for just the right moment to attack Blake, he was getting goosebumps. He shivered and started to approach the gleaming horse. Just 3 more steps and he could claim the horse, and all his hard work would be finally paid off. But then he froze in his tracks. A memory just hit him like an arrow, as if his brain wanted him to remember something. The memory was about a class he had at the camp. The class was about classifying monsters and identifying superpowers. Most of the monsters and heroes, had a forte of acting like a chameleon. Camouflaging to their respective backgrounds. The camouflaged so well that it was almost invisible to the naked eye unless you were looking straight at that monster. If you were, then you would notice tiny details. Like if a pattern was being followed in the background, it would be slightly broken, or the the background wouldn't look real. Blake thought of the best place to camouflage. It should be such a place in which Blake can't see them. So his back of his head should be clearly visible to the camouflager, he purposely dropped his sword. He slowly turned to pick up his sword, while doing that he looked around the whole room. The best place to camouflage would be next to the doorway. He peered closely at it, sure enough, he noticed tiny details like broken backgrounds and the wall looked kind of 3D. He got up and looked at the wall something shifted, probably the guy was nocking an arrow. He waited for about a second, he knew the guy was going to shoot his head. He waited for another second, and then he ducked, the arrow whizzed past him. If he would have waited for another millisecond, the arrow would have hit him. He looked at the person, and he froze. It was the last person he was expecting the person to be. The mysterious camouflager was none other than, his best buddy Goat. He had no clue how the Goat had entered the camp past all that security and stuff, but he knew why he was here. Blake knew he couldn't take the goat down 1 on 1. He was already exhausted and how much ever the Goat acted dumb. He was indeed really powerful, so the best idea currently was to stall the Goats plan to kill him. And wait for the perfect chance to strike when the Goat is distracted. Blake began "Hey buddy, what's up, seen you after a long time. Oh nice kicks by the way." The Goat knew it was a trick, but he couldn't help talking about shoes, so he began. "Oh these, I got them from the Adidas showroom in Boston. Man I really love these", and so for about 15 mins Blake and the Goat chatted about shoes. Football and why Avengers infinity wars was one of the best movies created. The Goat became so comfortable, he sat on the ground and started talking. Blake just waited for more time and then finally he said "Hey man, can you just pass me my water bottle its right behind you." "Sure pal." The Goat replied. He was just about to pass him his water bottle when Blake took out his sword and slashed him. The Goat howled in pain and shock, but mostly in betrayal. The Goat fell to his knees, and he started disintegrating. But before he could disintegrate he said "Subscribe to my youtube channel at least."

"Sure pal," Blake replied. After the goat had disintegrated. Blake went over to the golden horse and touched it. It glowed brighter for a second, and then it burst into light. After a few seconds when Blake was done rubbing out the spots from his eyes. He saw an eagle land next to him, Amber and Oscar came running down the stairs and immediately embraced Blake. Amber had tears of happiness, and Oscar was laughing aloud. They climbed onto the Eagle, and they headed back into the camp where everyone congratulated them. After that they had in the hall where their whole performance was broadcasted to all the campers. They gasped and cheered when they saw Blake defeat those duos with his powers. But as soon as the part came were the Goat had confronted him, The whole video shut. The technical guy came and said it was a glitch. And now the whole hard drive is spoilt. But Blake new why the Goat didn't want anyone to know that it had breached the defences of the camp, or else they would increase security and the other pathways to the camp, (which the monsters have found) would be sealed. Blake was willing to bet that there were already a handful of monsters here at camp. Spying on there every move and getting more monsters to infiltrate the camp. But these were purely assumptions. Currently he was enjoying the lavish dinner here at camp.

"It happens Blake, you know why we did that," said Master Domo. "So that I don't miss my parents and get attuned to the surroundings is your brilliant excuse for putting a forgetting charm on me?" Said Blake. "Blake listen, the time of the outside world is much slower than this dimension. So when you go back into your world, the events of your world would be same, example. We picked you up when you were in the museum right? So when you go back into your world, you would be at the museum, the same as you left. So currently in your world nothing is happening, but as soon as you go into your world, tie will start running again." said Master Domo. "Fine!" Replied Blake, but he was still astonished by what he was hearing. He headed over to to the breakfast table, today was his big day, it was the first time he was going on a quest. He sat next to Oscar and Amber, they were going to finalise on their route plan and then submit it to the committee for approval. Amber took out a piece of paper, "This is our rough plan, I'm going to take you guys once more through this, and just tell me if anything is wrong. So that we can edit it."Said Amber. Blake and Oscar nodded their heads. "So,we are first going to go to the mountain Doom, where we're going to get some of the dark elixirs after that were going to mix that into the hue potion I'm carrying. So that we don't get any side effects lingering near the Portal. After doing that were going to go to the forbidden place, get a map to the portal, get the portal crystal, and then use the gem portal to get quickly to camp." Completed Amber. Oscar raised his hand and said "I have a question if we can use the gem to come back to the camp without flying why can't we use it to go to the mountain and everywhere else?" Amber replied "It's because we can only use it once, and it would be best to use it when we have the portal stone in possession because all of the soldiers of the ruler would be attacking us. Therefore using the gem portal would be the easiest and safest way for us to come back to camp with ought them catching us. And also, when we use the gem portal, we cannot be tracked, so the camps location would be unknown." "I think that's a great plan." Said Oscar, eyeing Ambers chicken sandwich. "Okay then, I'll go to the council and submit the plans." As soon as amber was out of sight Oscar grabbed the sandwich and took a big bite out of it, Blake sighed in disbelief.

"Nice strike, Blake." Said master Wong, the teacher of the advanced sword fight-class. Blake was actually kind of surprised that he had reached the advanced stage of the sword fighting class in about a month. But he was the saviour, so he was naturally gifted. He gave a hand to Oscar who lay sprawled across the floor groaning and wincing in pain. Oscar grabbed Blades hand and tore himself from the floor with great difficulty. "Okay kids, 15 mins of break time" Oscar and Blake went to sit, "How did you get so good at sword fighting?" Said Oscar " Well, practice makes you perfect." Blake replied with a grin, he was actually happy that someone was praising him for the first time. He looked at his watch, and sighed "Amber told us to be at the council by 2:30, and it's already 2:45." Blake exasperated, "Hey why are you looking at me like that man, you know I'm bad with keeping track of time." said Oscar, Blake rolled his eyes, They headed out towards the council's wing not knowing what awaited them.

Chapter 12

They entered inside the room called "Important Council meetings." The room was pretty normal, and regular sized. It was surrounded by weird artefacts and a big chest in the middle, the chest was on top of a large smooth concrete. The chest was faded, and all the shine had drained out from it. Amber was fiddling with a key with Master Domo besides her. "There is a golden sphere inside this chest, this is going to show you three possible outcomes of this war were going to have. This is just a small fraction of all the possibilities are there, but we sadly can't see all because this sphere requires enormous amounts of energy. That we really don't have." Said Amber, Blake was just thinking that was the magic ball eight he used to use, just a rip-off of this golden sphere. But he had more pressing matters to think about like let's say, the end of the universe. Amber spoke a little more about how it's dangerous to see all possibilities in the future because it can actually alter the future if you know it. Blake was just focusing on his sword, the more he thought about it, the more confident he became. This was no ordinary sword, and the centre of the sword contained nothing but "Blake!" Shrieked Amber "Yeah I'm listening."

Replied Blake Amber was furious, she always spoke nicely to others but man. When she had a bad temper she erupted like a volcano thought Blake. She replied "You do understand that the fate of the universe rests in you hand doesn't it." Blake looked tense, he looked at the sword and blurted out "This is a power source isn't it?" Amber and Master Domo's expression darkened. "We didn't want to tell you till you were ready, or else you would freak out." "I understand." Said Blake "It's completely okay, I'll do my best. And hey, I don't want to look at a bunch of possibilities, I want to just do my best, and if i succeed or don't succeed it depends on me." Amber nodded her head "I completely understand Blake, now let's go and get that portal to the power source."

Blake was bored and cold as the icy cold wind hitting his face at about 50 miles per hour. He was also scared about toppling over from the dragon which was soaring above the clouds. Amber was sitting in front of him while Oscar was sitting behind him and snoring. Gigantic, enormous mountains loomed around him. The pitch dark night contrasted with the misty blueish clouds hanging above. Blake was just about to take a nap when Amber exclaimed Look, that's the mountain of Doom!" Blake immediately looked at the direction Amber was pointing that mountain made the other mountains look like atoms. It was the most enormous mountain Blake had seen. Purplish hue of smoke rose above the sizzling crater.

The whole peak radiated fear and well, the possibility of Doom. As they approached the mountain, Blake could see streams of lava. Well what looked like lava except it was a black and with wisps of purple smoke rising from it. They landed near the edge of the mountain, the terrain was rocky, but they finally managed to get the hang of it. They climbed to the nearest stream and Amber took out a bottle of a glowing blue liquid she mixed some of the streams liquid with the bottle. Now they solution glowed a tint of dark blue. She did this with three bottles. She two to Blake and Oscar and kept one with herself, before drinking she said. "This would save us from harmful magic and would not cause any side effects from holding to the portal stone." They nodded their heads in a silent agreement and Drank. Blake's throat burned, he knelt down clutching his shirt. He looked at his hands, they were turning a shade of purple. For a second he thought Amber got the solution wrong. But then he felt much better, his sleepiness went away. His hands returned to their normal shade, and in fact, he felt more aware of his surroundings. It was like now sensed everything around him. He looked at Amber and Oscar, they were looking around too, they smiled at each other and headed back towards the dragon. Blake was pleased, he thought this quest would be tougher, with some kind of people guarding the mountain but this was actually really easy. He looked around, no threats, nothing. "This was actually really easy, I mean no monsters attacked us." Amber looked around, and said "Blake its best not to speak anything until we get back to the dragon and we have flown far away." Oscar joined in and said "Yes I mean nothing happened, no ones here." Amber gave a stern look to Oscar, so he just smirked.

Chapter 13

They were just about to step onto the dragon when a huge gust of wind knocked them. Blake looked surprised, he looked around there was no one, then just behind him 4 people materialised. They all had humanoid faces, but they were much taller with elf like noses. They had a hideous smirk on their faces, one of them stepped forward and hissed "What a wonderful surprise, At last someones here, now we can capture them and make them are slaves." "Like that gonna happen." Said Amber, she looked at Oscar handed him the vial and firmly said "Go keep this safely in my bag, which is hung on the dragon. He will keep it safe." Oscar nodded and sprinted towards the dragon. All 4 of the creatures closed in. "We are the elves, you entered our territory, now you won't be leaving it." Said the elves rasping in unison. Amber materialised two pocket knives, glowing a harsh shade of red. Blake concentrated and materialised a sword glowing bright orange. The elves separated, two of them went to amber while the other two came to Blake. The Blake leaped forward and slashed onto one of the elves. He dodged and hit Blake on the back with one of the rods he had, the rod glowed bright purple. Blake grunted and again came to hit on of the elves, the elf jumped behind Blake just as he was about to hit. Blake ducked, and the elf missed. But now instead of hitting the same elf Blake quickly turned and slashed on the face of the other elf. The other elf was not aware of what's happening he fell screaming as his body slowly disintegrated. The other elf jabbed Blake on the stomach, and he crumpled. He was groaning in pain when a Blast of pure light attacked the elf. The elf screamed its body disintegrating. Blake looked at the direction at which the light came from, he saw Oscar standing there rubbing his hands Oscar looked bored and casual and said "I was bored." "Show off!" Blake replied. Oscar just grinned he looked at Amber. She had already taken down one elf but was struggling with the other. She slashed out with her knife, the elf dodged, twisted, jumped and hit her with his rod. Amber fell, hitting a boulder. Blake thought of an ideal weapon for the situation, and the first thing that came into his mind was a dagger. He concentred, and slowly a dagger materialised into his hand glowing orange. He threw it with immense force, the dagger whistled and hit the elf in the head. The elf collapsed. Blake headed out to help Amber. He walked by the elf, and the elf said "You might have one the war now, but when the ruler of all, gets his hands on all crystals you will perish." With that the elf turned into dust. Blake sighed in frustration. He helped Amber to get up, "You okay ?" said Blake "I have never felt better." Replied Amber. They quietly headed up towards the dragon. "We go to the forbidden place right?" said

Oscar Amber nodded. "I have a question, What exactly does the stone portal do?" "I knew you would ask that question sometime or later." Said amber. "The stone portal basically teleports you to the dimension in which the specific crystal is kept. Currently there are 4 crystals, that means there are 4 portal stones teleporting you to 4 different dimensions. But the dimensions aren't that big, like our dimension or the frost dimension. They are just about as big as a small garden and circular in shape. They have a box in the middle where the crystal is kept. The crystal which you have located in the hilt of your sword also came from 1 of the four dimensions. The portal stone however of your dimension is safely kept in a secure place." Replied Amber. "so basically the ruler is going after the portal stone to get the crystal" said Blake. Amber nodded, "but what do these crystals do?" Asked Oscar. "even I don't know that, I only know these things because I have stayed in this camp the longest." "well, we all will ask Master Domo about our doubts, for now we have a mission to complete," said Blake. They all nodded, and they flew high into the paint splattered sky.

"We stop here for resting." Amber climbed out of the dragon. "Does he have a name?" Blake asked "Yes, his name is blacklight" replied Oscar who was slowly removing his sandwich out of the foil, "you want a bite?" Asked Oscar. Blake nodded Oscar gave a small piece of only bread to Blake. Blake rolled his eyes. "He just loves eating" amber sighed. Oscar continued to chew on his sandwich with delight. "is there like a hotel or something we can stay in?" Asked Blake. "no need, I got this" she removed a piece of circular paper and threw it, as soon as they the paper touched the ground, it inflated into a large circular type tent. "wow" Blake gasped in awe he entered the tent. It was much bigger in the inside than on the outside, which Blake new was a type of illusion. "they tent can also be folded back into its original shape and has multiple layers of security so no intruder can get inside" said Amber. Blake walked around the tent. It had everything a TV, a refrigerator stocked with snacks and packed water bottles, to a couch and also it had a TT table. "How is this stuff possible?" Blake asked his eyes gleaming like glass marbles. "well, at the camp we have multiple engineers and mechanics who use some illusion magic, and other stuff at camp to create these kinds of things, most of our weapons and robotic guards are also manufactured by them, in fact when most of them leave for summer, they work at top tech companies like Apple, Space x etc." said Amber "Well this is great, I'll see you in the morning." Amber said goodnight to him and shut the door. Blake went and sat on the couch. He summoned his sword, It immediately appeared with calm blue light in his hand. He looked at the hilt of his sword. The gem was glowing blue. He tried to focus his energy into the sword. He intensely concentrated, his palms turning warm. He waited, but nothing happened. He sighed with exhaustion. The gem just glowed brighter for a few seconds before returning to its original state. Blake grabbed a blanket and dozed off.

"Sir, we have found the location." A voice hissed, submerged in darkness. "And we also have a plan to ambush the team. Soon they will come to the forbidden place where they will seek the map of the portal stone, we have one of our men placed there which will ambush them." "Very well, go and bring the portal stone to me." A deep voice boomed. The man was wearing a type of bronze helmet which covered his face. "Okay sir, we shall start our journey in a couple of hours." "Take the general with you." The man with the mask who sat on the throne said.

"Man I'm feeling so sleepy." Oscar said "What is with you, were on a mission to save multi-dimensions one which includes earth, and you're telling me your feeling sleepy?" said Amber rolling her eyes. "Keep rolling your eyes, maybe you'll find a brain back in there, or maybe you won't." Said Oscar snickering Amber glared at Oscar. Her fierce eyes burning, her face looked like she could kill somebody, well, if somebody counted as "Oscar". "Sorry!" Said Oscar a little bit frightened and shaken. It was crystal clear that Oscar was pretty scared of Amber, given the things she could do. Like shoot 3 arrows at once or throw a couple of daggers with ought even having to move a muscle. That was really scary. Sure, even Blake and Oscar could materialise their own weapons. But to control them with the same level of concentration Amber uses with ought breaking a sweat of moving a muscle... Just with the help of her mind, was something which takes years of training. "If you are done with your little argument, could we proceed to plan out how were goanna get the map from the forbidden place?" Said Blake, expectantly waiting. "Fine I'll start." Amber pulled out a folder from her bag and put it on the breakfast table next to her half eaten sandwich. "So basically, the forbidden place is on earth, It's an aquarium." "What! I thought the forbidden place was like in a whole other dimension, with like a scary castle and looming mountains and a dark sky, you know the whole scary package." Said Oscar clearly disappointed. "Anyway, in the forbidden place, there is a guy from our camp named Alex who is working undercover there, coincidentally he found the map about weeks ago in the ocean when he went to look for rare fishes. He has kept the map with him, and I have contacted him so he will gladly give us the map." Amber said with excitement. "Well that's great then, what are we waiting for?" Said Blake enthusiastically getting up from his chair.

Chapter 14

New York City was bustling with people. Blake lived in New Jersey but had visited New York once or twice. But he had never visited New York in a flying dragon on a quest to save the world. They got down on the top of the building. Luckily no one saw them. They walked for about 10 minutes and then they found the "Forbidden Aquarium." Amber paid for the three of them for the pass, she had packed money just in case.

They entered the aquarium; enormous tanks filled with sea green water surrounded them. There were multiple fishes of every kind there. Blake also saw a huge hammer headed shark which was going around in loops inside the water. "There he is!" Amber pointed to one of the staff who was wearing a badge that said "Alex!" on it. He was a rather short guy who was bald with a golden overflowing moustache. He looked like the hammer headed shark Blake had just seen. Amber went to him and whispered something in his ear. He looked at Blake and Oscar and motioned them to follow him. The three of them went after him. Blake couldn't help but notice that something was weird about this guy. The way he was nervously looking around and tapping his gun. He got them into a room which was quite huge. There were cleaning supplies everywhere, and old papers work was strewn around. "Okay so where is the map, Alex?" Amber asked Blake knew even she was feeling a bit suspicious. Alex's expression darkened with a grim look he said "I am sorry Amber, but It's for the best." Suddenly 2 men wearing coats descended, They literally descended, there were wings attached to the back of the men, and instead of teeth they had sharp. Deadly fangs stuck to their mouths, they looked at them with bloodshot eyes. "Okay so we have a janitor and 2 people straight out from vampire diaries to deal with, not bad." Said Blake materialising 2 concentric spinning discs in each hand glowing bright blue. Ambers pulled out two daggers from her back pocket and glared at the vampires or whatever they were. Oscar, well he threw the wrapper of his sandwich in a bin. Chewed whatever he had for some time. Took out a napkin wiped his mouth and then said "I am ready." "Seriously you're not gonna use a weapon or something." Asked Blake wondering if he needed the help of psychiatrist or something "Just wait and watch." Said Oscar with a grin. The two vampires came charging at Blake and Oscar. Alex pulled out a sword which shows just how bad the security was at this aquarium and charged at Amber. Blake threw one disc at the vampire, the vampire dodged flew and landed a kick on Blake's face, Blake defended it with the other disc, the disc he threw came at him like a boomerang, but instead of aiming it at the vampire,

Blake willed the disc to come at him, as soon as it came at him, Blake jumped on it, using the disc as a platform he leaped, twisted in mid-air, materialised a bright orange sword and slashed the monster with it, this all happened within seconds. The monster crumpled and evaporated. He saw Oscar, to his surprise, Oscars hands were glowing bright golden. He was using this to punch the vampire, but this vampire was fast, he dodged all of his strikes and managed to hit Oscar on the face, Oscar fell, just as the monster was about to tear Oscar into pieces, Blake kicked the vampire, The vampires hit one of the bundles of paper work and snarled "what you don't like to do paper work, buddy, bet you don't like to turn into dust either" said Blake throwing a Disc at him, The vampire dodged and did something unexpected, it materialised a ball of flame and threw it at Blake, Blake didn't have the time to dodge it, so he used the disc as a shield, as soon as the ball collided with the disc, it exploded into a column of flames, tearing down the wall behind Blake and knocking over several boxes. Blake went flying into the gap of the broken wall, he found himself next to the aquarium of the hammer head shark he was seeing. He groaned and tried to get up but the monster landed on him and dug its talons into Blake's arm and said "This is for the greater good, now we creatures will live in freedom instead of hiding in shadows, we will rule all over earth and the other dimensions" Blake saw a glimpse of Oscar running and jumping behind the vampire, he landed on the vampire grabbed its neck, twisted him and gave him a punch, the monster went flying breaking the wall. Oscar helped Blake get up. Then through the area of broken wall and rubble, the vampire came flying. Before Blake could process what is happening the vampire grabbed Oscars neck and slammed him to the glass of one of the aquarium. The vampire opened its mouth to breath fire, but Oscar managed to twist and punch the monster one more time. Exploding the glass behind them. All the water from the aquarium came gushing out, alarms were ringing, and people were running here and there. But no one came near their path which was good. Blake tried to escape the wrath of the water but he too along with Oscar and the vampire were swallowed into the rapacious currents. Water was gushing around them everywhere filling the whole aquarium and breaking other tanks to because of the pressure. Blake held tried to swim to the other part of the aquarium the open the main door, so the water flushes out, he could see it. It was about 50 meters away, but just as he was about to reach the aquarium, the vampire landed on him, choking him. He couldn't breathe at all, his whole body was shivering, his chest was burning his eyes were shutting, he was losing consciousness. But suddenly Oscar came grabbed the vampire and threw it to one of the other walls. Blake swam up, breathed some air and again came underwater. He materialised a disc and threw it at the vampire, this time the vampire was too busy chasing Oscar underwater. The disc curved and it hit the vampire, the vampire twisted and hit the main exit. Oscar saw this as his chance. He immediately swam near to the monster his fist glowing bright golden. And before the vampire could see what is happening,

Oscar punched it! Exploding the door and sucking all the water outside on the street.

Chapter 15

Blake ended up on the sidewalk soaked to the bone in the water he was shivering, Oscar lay beside him trying to get up. Amber came running to them and said "Where have you to been?" "Swimming I guess," said Oscar. The sounds of sirens were approaching closer to them. "Let's go now, I got the map." Said Amber the dragon flew onto the sidewalk. With manysurprising tourist reactions, they climbed onto the dragon and flew away.

Blake woke up with a start, his hair was all ruffled up and flying. He realised he had been so exhausted that he had slept on the dragon itself. He was sitting near the tail of the dragon. Ahead him sat Oscar, who was also snoring away. Ahead of him sat amber who was steering the Dragon. The dragon slowly descended losing altitude. Blake could make out mountains, valleys and the glittering and shimmering ocean. He realised this area was kind of familiar "Hey where are we going." Said Blake. Amber looked behind and said "To camp, councils orders." Blake looked surprised and also kind of disappointed but managed a low nod. Blake just looked at the horizon, he was feeling dejected. The only thing which he had ever been handed responsibility was now being snatched away from him. He could make out sharks, birds and other stuff, but something caught his eye. It was a large bird, as it approached them. Blake could make out that the object was not a bird but a dragon, with two people on it. It looked like the dragon was following them before Blake could make out what is happening or tell Amber. Black light took a considerable dip, lowering their altitude by about 1,500 meters. The other dragon followed. Blake looked behind, the dragon opened its mouth, and a huge fireball came out of it Blake yelled "Jump! Now!" he grabbed Oscar who was yet sleeping. After about seconds Amber also jumped. The dragon might have sensed what is happening, so it tilted sideways, missing the fireball narrowly. Blake, Amber and Oscar were now airborne. Falling at 90 km plummeting to their deaths.

Blake woke up with a start. His eyes were burning, and he coughed out seawater. His muscles were all sore. He looked around himself, he was lying on a beach surrounded by campers and medics. Amber and Oscar lay beside him. Master Domo was nearby discussing something with the council members. Blake slowly and shakily got up, he spat a few times so that he could get rid of the taste of sand. The medics wanted to tend to Blake but he just politely told them no. He wanted to first ask with Master Domo why he couldn't continue with the mission. Amber and Oscar were also fine, they just had some minor cuts, but they were okay. Blake asked Amber how they survived the crash, Amber said that as soon as they fell in the sea. 3 sea horses saved them by taking on their impact and immediately rushing them to the shore. Also, the sea had magical properties which boosted oneself healing, so that helped them too. After that the medics took care of the by some advanced level healing magic which could not be matched even by modern medicine. Blake looked towards the sea, the three gigantic sea horses where doing summersaults in the water and enjoying themselves. He headed towards his room.

Blake quickly changed and headed up towards the council. Apparently even they wanted to meet with them. Blake entered inside the big building, made up of entirely white marble. He went towards the desk manager who beamed when he saw Blake. " I have got an appointment for today 3:00 clock with the council." said Blake "Okay, the council will see you now." Blake entered the massive room, it was an oak style room with everything made up of wood. The main committee sat in the centre in a semi-circle. The rest of the people sat in front of them with desks. On that desks there was a note pad, pen and a glass of water and the respective person's name. Blake found his name tag on a desk between Amber and Oscar. He saw many familiar faces like the strategic war department sitting in the next door and also Master Domo who sat with the committee. "Let us proceed with the meeting."

Said Master Domo. "As most of you know, there has been a certain crisis which has arisen. The ruler is back." Many of the campers gasped "Well last time he was not fully killed." Continued Master Domo. "This time he will not only go for the 4 crystals, but he is also planning something else. We do not know what he is doing, but It's something big but looking on the bright side. He is not capable of doing it himself at least not now, he is still recovering from last times war. This would take him quite some time." mutters and whispers could be heard from almost all campers. "Well, we had to call off the mission early was because we received a prophecy." Continued Master Domo. "The prophecy was apparently locked up in a chest and thrown into the sea. It was waiting for someone to open it during this time. I shall now read the prophecy." Everyone was surprised now because if the prophecy was terrible, you were doomed. You couldn't escape a prophecy, it always came true. "The ruler of all men shall go to the darkest of hell." Read Master Domo "To get the most precious gem of them all. He who has the blessed blade shall stand over the crystals tall. He shall end the greatest of all fight. With enormous might It shall be either of the two who pierce the blade in the dragon's heart. Now for the second part of the prophecy, with all crystals the ruler ends all, only either of the two can save the world by sacrificing, and making themselves fall."

The whole crowd was awestruck, each of them started blabbering and talking loudly. Blake put his hand on his forehead. He was feeling like the whole world was spinning, he thought he was safe because he would be the one completing the prophecy. But now there was another person in the prophecy that meant one of them needed to die. "Silence." Master Domo said "I am sure many of you are interpreting the prophecy, but with prophecies you can never be sure. Prophecies give us two realities of what's going to happen. But that depends on the person who is in the prophecy, how strong his will to fight is, that is what it all boils down to. There is a war coming, and to win it we got to be strong. Supportive and the most important of all, never lose the will to fight. We currently don't know who the second person in the prophecy is, maybe there is no second person, that doesn't matter, we will all together be strong." Suddenly the whole mood of the place changed, people started standing up and clapping. Even Blake felt a little better, but still he couldn't shrug off the feeling that there is a second person.

The group ate in silence, none of them said a word to each other. Amber was angry, Oscar was dejected. And well Blake was just a tiny bit relieved that this whole quest thing was over, now in about 2 weeks he could go home start with his normal lifestyle like going to school. Meeting with friends playing Fortnite and as much as Blake hated to say it. He was kind of missing all the HW he used to do at night. The way he used to study for his exams, he was just missing his whole routine, and he wanted to go home so badly and just pretend this was some sort of bad dream and forget about it. He didn't want to risk saving his life for the universe or anything like that. He was just a normal kid who went to middle school.

"I can't believe the committee aborted our mission, we were doing so well. I mean we just had to make one last stop, and then we would have got that stone" "Amber It's okay!" Said Oscar "They are just sending another more experienced team than us because the committee was concerned about Blake's safety. Because in the end when the last prophecy starts to unravel, Blake and that other guy will be needed." Blake just stared at his potatoes. "But you know, only we can complete this right, even the prophecy says so."

Said Amber "Amber we can't do anything about this." "Unless, we can who says we need to do what the committee exactly says, I mean the fate of all dimensions rest on our shoulder, we need to do what's practical." Said Amber "I know what you are thinking" said Oscar with a grin "And I'm in!" They looked at Blake expectantly for an answer, "Look, guys, I'm all in for kicking monsters and saving the multiverse and stuff like that, but I got to put my foot down here." Said Blake " Look, even I have got a life okay, I want to go back to school, meet with my family and friends, preferably in one piece. This saving the universe thing is just too big a responsibility for me. I am in middle school." Amber sighed "Look if you don't want to go, that's fine but remember. How will you meet with your friends, family go to school if there will be none of that? You know very well what the ruler will do once he gets his hands one all crystals. He will infiltrate every dimension, destroy it, and turn it into his own. We will go, with or with ought you. We will leave camp at the crack of dawn, you know where to find us."

Chapter 16

Blake couldn't sleep, he kept contemplating about the wether he did the right thing or no. But by morning, he had made his decision. He left a little note on his bed and headed out to eat breakfast. He ate rather quickly, he immediately finished took his backpack from his room and headed out towards the farm where the dragon Blacklight stayed. There were many other exotic animals including a flying horse with a horn. He wondered if humans got the idea of a unicorn from here. He met Oscar and Amber near the unicorn stables. Oscar was eating a sandwich naturally, and Amber was petting the dragon. "We knew you would come." Said Amber, Blake just nodded. They sat on the dragon and flew away from the camp, Blake clung on to dear life. "Well the man we got from the aquarium was actually useless." Said Amber "It was a fake map, the real map was with the vampires who we met with. and the map which was with them got destroyed after the big explosion Oscar caused in the aquarium" "Then how will we know where the stone is ?" Asked Oscar "Well I found out about a guy who was present at the time of the last war, after the portal stones were restored he saw one stone fall from the sky, that means he knows the location of the stone." Said Amber "But how is that possible? The war was about 150 years ago. How is this guy still alive?" Said Blake "Well this guy has been alive for about 300 years, and still continues to live because he drinks the immortal syrup." Said Amber "Could I get like a glass of that too, immortality doesn't sound so bad you know." Said Oscar "You can't, because that drink is made only for celestial and minor celestial beings." Said Amber "Who are those?" Asked Blake "Celestial and minor celestial beings are those beings who were born when time had recently started. Celestial beings were first after that came the minor celestial beings. There were a total of 5 celestial beings who crafted their own powers into 5 powerful objects, those 5 powerful objects came to be known as the crystals. But soon a huge war broke out between them, they used their crystals to destroy each other, the war lasted 500 years, at the end all of them died. The crystals were put to 5 different dimensions, and the minor celestial beings swore to protect it. The first generation of minor celestial beings crafted out these portal stones to reach the crystals when they needed them. Now there are many minor celestial beings like Master Domo. The ruler and the guy who we are going to meet, but they are like the 50th generation of them." Said Amber "Oh." Blake remarked. "The problem is many of the celestial beings are siding with the ruler, so he's going to have a huge army that is really dangerous for us." Said Amber "But why are some minor beings siding with the ruler." "Because they are this cousin his own brothers, if you think about it, all of us are related." Blake felt like he had been hit on the face "what how are all of us related ?" "Well all our moms and dads are either minor beings, which is rare, or they are related to them. Like my mom is a minor celestial being, but my dad is not, so I am half a celestial being, same with Oscar but with you. It's different both your parents are minor celestial beings, which makes you a proper minor celestial being" Said Amber "I didn't know that, I mean no one told me." Said Blake "We wanted to wait for the right time Blake." said Amber. Blake just nodded, he decided to accept this twisted reality in which he lived and decided to concentrate on the mission. "We will be reaching our destination in about 3 hours. You guys can nap if you need cause It's gonna be a long and deadly journey ahead" said Amber. They glided past the glittering sea, thinking if they would see it again.

Blake woke up with blurry eyes, everything was out of focus, Amber and Oscar had both woken up, but he couldn't make out their faces. He rubbed his eyes, no luck, everything still seemed pixelated. After some time, he realised it was not his eyes, but there was immense fog outside. It was so thick that whenever they went past one, he could actually touch it. The scenery looked like giant marshmallows and cotton candy strewn around. They glided below the fog, and now Blake could see clearly, he saw looming mountains, they shade of dark purple, contrasting with the bright pink rivers flowing downstream. He saw clouds, the colour of pink, purple and light blue. Overall, this place looked straight out of an animated movie. But Blake wasn't surprised at all, he thought partly the reason for this was that when you start seeing flying dragons. Vampires and the fate of the universe lay in your hands, you tend to become a bit used to your daily surroundings. "There, that's where our guy lives." Said Amber pointing to a small grey hut. Blacklight slowly descended in an ark towards the hut. The small grey hut kind of stood out from the background a bit. It felt like it had been power washed, draining all the colour from its wall. Blacklight landed just in front of the hut. They slowly climbed out of the dragon, they approached the hut very carefully, looking for any traps or some vampires or something. Blake swore he heard someone saying "Go, Cristiano! score that goal!" Amber knocked on the door, no one answered she just opened the door and froze. Blake quickly followed and to his bewilderment. He found out the man he was looking at was well, normal, the man looked like an average human. He didn't have a flaming sword, or a grand chariot or anything like that. He was a regular guy sitting in front of the T.V watching football with a can of soda. "My lord." Said Amber immediately bowing down and signalling Blake and Oscar to also do the same. "Well, well what do we have hear, two half-celestial beings and one full celestial beings." Blake looked surprised, he hadn't told this guy that he was a complete celestial being. "You have come for a quest I presume." "Yes my lord, we have come here to know the whereabouts of the portal stone." Said Amber. "Well I'm sorry, I can't help you. Many centuries ago I swore never to tell the whereabouts of any portal stone after the havoc it had caused. So I'm sorry hero's, but your quest ends here." With that he turned his eyes towards the television and continued to watch the match. "Well, you have got to help us, I mean the whole fate of universe rests on us, and you are just saying you cannot help us because of some promise you made. Just think for a moment, if the ruler succeeds, none of us will survive. And also you won't be able to see your little match on the T.V, so you better make a choice now Demos." Said Blake getting up. Demos glared at Blake, Blake could make out tiny wisps of fire in his eye. The room became freezing. It was feeling like Demos was pouring all his anger out on the air, the table began to rattle. Blake heard thunder booming in the sky, it was feeling like there was an earth- quake. Blake tried his level best to maintain balance. "Well" said Demos, rather calmly. The room came to its normal temperature, and the thunder and earthquake stopped. "Nobody has called me by my real name in decades, cause not many people know it. But now, after you said my name, I realised who you are. But I will only help you in one condition, I need favour so will you accept it the chosen one." Blake started to feel giddy, for some reason he started to see scenes of battle raging. He saw glimpses, but he felt weird. "I know what you are feeling." Said Demos, "Some pieces of memory from the last crystal user are transplanted in your head. It's really rare, but it happens, now since I know how important you are. I'll help you, but I need you to do something for me first." "Name it." Said Amber

"We will do it." Blake looked at Amber thinking if it was such a good idea Amber stuck to her decision. Demos smiled coldly "It's the type of heroes. They make a promise they won't be able to complete. Just telling you this is an impossible task, only two people in the past have been able to do it." "Name it, we aren't just called heroes."

Said Blake Demos smiled. Blake was getting tired of walking, they were walking for an hour and the more they walked. The more dangerous the terrain became, well, because it was a mountain and they were walking uphill. At one point Oscar almost slipped and was about to tumble down the mountain, luckily Amber quickly grabbed him. "I really don't know why we're doing this." Said Oscar "I mean there is surely some other way we could have got the map, maybe we could have forced him to give us the map, he was outnumbered, and he didn't look really powerful." "Oscar Demos is one of the oldest celestial beings, even though his powers have faded through the centuries, he still remains really powerful." Said Amber "Even though he was outnumbered, he could take us all and not break a sweat." "Fine," Oscar replied.

"But seriously, why does he want us to check if anyone is stealing some of the immortality drink." Said Blake "I mean a couple of people drinking it wouldn't hurt anyone." "Blake the immortality drink does not only give people immortality powers, but it could be forged to create something compelling. Like a weapon which could destroy cities and cause havoc." Said Amber "Well, why can't he just go and check it himself ?" Asked Oscar "Well because they will sense his presence and run away like they always do. That is also the reason why we can't fly our dragon up on the mountain" Said Amber. "Umm guys, you got to see this." Said Amber. She had reached the rim of the mountain first and was staring around it Blake, and Oscar quickly scrambled on top.

What Blake was seeing was just beyond imagination, he had never seen anything like this is his whole life. The whole life also included his partly crazy life were he had to save the world and stuff. The whole mountain was actually a whole active volcano. But this was not like ordinary volcanoes you see. The lava oozing out of different craters in the volcano was actually purple in colour with bright splotches of red and orange. The whole rim volcano was covered with a kind of transparent glass, but it was stronger than glass, because as soon as the volcano erupted. Lava came splashing on the glass, the glass didn't burn, but it became very hot. The erupted lava was then transported deeper inside the volcano with huge pipes made of chromium and coated with radon. One of the most powerful substances on earth.(He had learnt this at the classifying elements class at camp) There were many workers working on this project. Some looked human, others not so much. They ducked behind rim just as someone approached them from inside. They were just about to leave when Blake heard something. A monster with a rock like texture was talking to another guy dressed in neat formals.

They were talking about a godly weapon being made inside the forges with the help of the radon collected from the lava. They said something about liquid radon mixed with chromium and then radiated to a specific limit made the mixture the strongest on earth.

The monster with the rock texture told that the radiator was getting a bit out of control and it was giving more than the required energy. The man in the formals nodded and said he would go check into this matter. Blake explained this to Amber and Oscar. They knew what this meant. That the ruler was making weapons for the war, they needed more information on this so that they could then report it to the committee. And they all knew that the radiator they were using could be a portal stone, they needed to find out what it was. Ambers solution- following the guy dressed in formals. Thats what they ended up doing and then things got pretty bad.

Chapter 17

Steam curled up from the vents on the path. They were going inside a tunnel which was leading them deeper and deeper in the ground. Precious metals were embedded inside the walls of the tunnels. Blake felt like plucking one of the wall but then he realised that the tunnel was kind of imbalanced, and any movement might cause it to topple down, so decided against it. The deeper they went inside the tunnel, the hotter it became, Blake nearly collided with a guy coming out of the tunnel. The guy had 5 huge arms, a face of a bulldog and with the legs of a dragon. Just seeing him made Blake shiver. Luckily all of them were wearing an invisibility pendant. But that didn't stop monsters from sensing them. once in a while, one of the monsters coming in or out of the tunnel would stop in his tracks, sniff around and then continue walking. Even Mr. Formals would occasionally stop, look behind his shoulder as if he was being followed, and then continue to walk. Just as Blake was about to tell amber to turn back because they had seen enough, They entered a humongous room, The wall of the room were coated with chromium and platinum. In the centre of the room there was a bronze table with a crystal glass box covering an object. Blake couldn't make out what the object because it was throwing of immense amount of light. The object was sending out a beam of light across the room, into a kind of circular panel. There was a guy who looked partially humanoid, but instead of fingernails he had big sharp talons, and instead of normal white teeth, he had fangs. "Its becoming unstable, its soon going to come out in its pure form, we need a better place to keep it." Said Mr. Fangs "We will ask boss soon, but for now you have to contain it" Said Mr. Formals "You aren't getting it, in about 3 to 5 days its going to erupt and come out in its true form. When that happens its going to collapse the whole facility and make the mountain erupt. All the weapons which we have been working on will be destroyed" Said Mr. Fangs "Okay, okay I'll try to tell boss about this issue, but remember this. When it comes in its true form you must immediately hand it over to the boss, don't give it to anybody else, after it comes in its true form, then it will be the most valuable to us, do you understand?" Said Mr. formals "Yes, I do, and by the way i ordered for 5 reactors from Lucas corporation on earth, have they come?" Said Mr. Fangs clearly he was a scientist here. "Yes they have, now get back to work, the reactors are kept in the cupboard there." Said Mr. formals and went back in the tunnel. The thought that they were smuggling weaponry from earth made Blake feel worried. If they had a way to get to earth then people would not be safe. And if the ruler succeeds in his mission, he might take over earth too. Blake shuddered thinking about it. "Blake!

are you listening to me." Said Amber "What if that object in that glass is a portal stone? If it is then its really risky because. If the portal stone comes in contact with something that has high energy. Then it could erupt." "Oh no,don't worry." Said Blake "Master Domo took away the crystal from my blade and replaced it with a normal gem because it would have been risky. If I would have gone on the quest with it because it could have fallen into somebody else's hands." Amber nodded "So should we take the object?" Said Amber "What?" replied Oscar "Of course not, it's too dangerous to handle and plus we will get caught." "But it could benefit our camp." Said Amber just as Amber and Oscar were arguing they guy with the fangs came in. He sniffed around and said "Alright I know you're here, show yourselves up, you spies." Blake looked amber, he could tell what she was thinking, their cover was busted. And they could only escape this place if they fought. Blake quickly put the invisibility pendant in his pocket and pulled out a sword Amber pulled out a knife and Oscar took out his blazing fists. Together they charged.

For scientist fang was pretty good at fighting. He leaped across from cupboards, dodged strikes and even kicked Blake once or twice in the face. But still, they were doing pretty well. Oscar punched that guy a couple of times, and Amber threw materialised knives at him. Blake slashed at fangs with his sword, and he scored one hit. But it went horrible wrong when Fangs kicked Blake so hard he flew across the room and landed next to the cupboard. Fangs then somehow grappled Oscar and took him in a choke. Oscars's face was turning purple, and he had about 40 seconds before he got choked "You lose." Said fangs "You will never win this war, you will perish." Amber and Blake were at the opposite end of the room, they didn't have time to do anything. Everything was kind of going in slow-motion. Blake tried to get up and then heard a whiz in the air, Amber had thrown a dagger which was glowing purple. Fangs unfortunately dodged, he let go of Oscar and jumped the other side. Oscar gasped and spluttered. The dagger sailed, and it hit the crystal box. which exploded in a massive blast of light. Blake looked around terrified, the walls were peeling off, ceilings were crumbling and falling. They had 30 seconds at best to escape before this whole place erupted. Smoke spews off the floor, the volcano was now active. Siren alarms blared across the entire tunnel. In about a minute security guards who were like fangs rushed in with swords and daggers. All exits were blocked. They were trapped in the room with an object that was about to detonate in about 20 seconds.

Blake did the intelligent thing. He Froze. He knew time was ticking and either he would die by the explosion or the security guards will kill him. But he just couldn't react, he was frozen stiff. He glanced at the object. It was glowing a bit brighter, and it was starting to heat up the room. He glanced at Amber and Oscar. Both of them were trying to hold off the security guards. Oscars' face was pale from the choking, but he still managed to fight the security.

While Blake, the saviour of humanity was frozen in shock. He glanced at Fangs, He was walking around the glass box muttering. "No, no this can't be right, we are not meant to do teleport now, this is all going wrong." Suddenly an idea sparked in Blake's head. He regained his senses, and ran towards amber, on the way he slashed a monster with his sword and took the hilt of the sword and hit it over a guys head. He immediately collapsed. He reached towards amber and said two words "Teleportation now." She immediately understood and began to unpack her Bag. Blake stood infant of her like a Line of defence and began to attack any monsters who came near them. They had about 10 seconds now. The object began to shine brighter and began a satisfied hum. The glass box was shaking dangerously. Oscar was fighting a bunch of security guards with his hands, but he was outnumbered bad. And even he was getting tired and was losing the battle. Oscar punched a security guard, the guard dodged it and hit Oscar in the face with a shield. "Amber we got about 5 seconds, find the thing quick!" Blake said, disintegrating 2 monsters and kicking the third one.

"Got it!" Amber said, revealing a gemstone glowing bright orange. The cube was initially meant for them to use as soon as they got the portal stone, but now they needed to improvise. "OSCAR COME HERE!!! NOW!" Blake yelled, Oscar immediately looked at Blake and then the cube and understood what was happening. He punched the security guard who was pinning him with his glowing fists and then ran off the join, Blake and Amber. The box started glowing brighter and rising into the air, It shook dangerously and began sending out energy waves. "3 seconds left to detonate said fangs everyone take cover!" Yelled fangs and dived behind the cover. Just as Oscar leapt into the air amber threw the gemstone on the ground Creating bright orange smoke and Blake's vision dissolved in it.

Chapter 18

Blake was bored. He never thought that after all these crazy adventures he would actually be bored in any of them but watching demos unpack his cupboards for like 45 mins was pure boredom. Finally, after an eternity, Demos pulled out a piece of paper. "Finally" Demos exclaimed. "This map shows you the place from where you can find the map to the portal which will lead you to the dimension where the portal stone is hidden. From there seek king Icarus. Even he is a celestial being. He will give you the directions to the portal stone from there. Remember, on this quest you will face many challenges, yet your biggest challenge is yet to come, the final battle. As people like to call it, might be the end of humanity and other dimensions. You hold the fate to either save the world or destroy it" "thanks, some really motivational and reassuring words." Said Blake. "Oh I almost forgot." He pulled out 2 gemstones the same ones which the used back in the mountain or what was left of the mountain. The whole mountain had erupted causing huge debris to fall everywhere. The explosion killed hundreds of monsters and set back their little operation to save the world by a few months. "These teleportation gems are for you, remember just thin of the place you need to go and hit it against the floor, they will erupt and take you there." Said Demos. "Thanks." the three of them said in unison and headed out towards their dragon.

"Wonderful"

Would not be a word that Blake would use to describe this terrifying, delusional, fatal quest which he was leading. But he actually felt great to be back at New York City. After a bit of poking around for information from other half-celestial beings. They found out that the person who had the map was another half-celestial being who was located in one of the ships called sea-princess, in the harbour. They headed out towards the harbour but on the way they helped themselves with candy-floss. It felt good to be home. Blake had to constantly remind himself that he was on a quest, but form time to time he felt like visiting his parents and telling them it was okay. But he figured they would kind of guess that he was on a quest because even they too would have been on a quest sometime in their life. Blake was absent-mindedly walking when Amber yelled "Look there! that's the ship!" Blake looked the direction she was pointing in, there was a huge ship with the letters "Sea princess." Engraved on it. There was a rope attached to it, and before you knew it, Oscar was climbing it. Blake and Amber went after him, and soon they were on the too. The sea glittered like a thousand diamonds under the blazing hot sun. Blake looked around everyone was having a regular day, some were going to work, others were sitting around the park having a nice picnic. But none were on a dangerous quest to save the world except for Blake. Oscar and Amber. Just thinking of this made Blake homesick, but he had to concentrate on the quest.

"Come on guys we got to get directions to a portal." Said Amber casually as if someone would say they needed directions to a bookstore. "Come, follow me" a voice beamed. It was not a human but in fact, a giant bunny rabbit. Blake had blink his eyes several times to actually understand what he was seeing. This was not one of their classical monsters with huge talons and fangs this was, in fact, a large, enthusiastic pink bunny rabbit. Blake could tell Amber and Oscar were also having a hard time believing what they saw."Master Alex is located in room 72." Said the bunny with a smile. "Our main business is an adventure park called Rabbit adventure land, you can look at our brochure while we walk to his room." The bunny handed out 3 brochures to them. Blake looked at the cover-page, a cute photo of a bunny playing with a Child was shown with the words "A wholesome adventure for the family." Inscribed on the top. They walked in silence for about 5 mins after that. "So are you like a half- celestial being or what?" Asked Oscar breaking the silence. Amber glared at him clearly hinting at him that it was not the best thing to ask. The rabbit's expression darkened. He stopped and said. " A long time ago even I was a half- celestial being, I supported the celestial beings in the war against the ruler and his army. We call them dark beings now. After we won the war, I and my other half-celestial being companions got a little greedy. We tried to take the portal stones, but Demos found out about it, and he cursed us to take form in this hideous outfit. We are stuck in this giant bunny costume" Said Bunny. There was silence for about 5 seconds "But who cares! that was a long time ago, now come follow me." Blake looked suspiciously at the bunny but then decided to follow him. They reached room 72. And that is when the trouble started

The room would not describe the facility that Alex lived in. It was actually a whole floor that Alex occupied. There were many lights dazzling across the ceiling with Italian flooring and huge carpets. There were many painting lined up along the wall, and one suspiciously looked like Mona Lisa. Blake decided not to ask if that was stolen or was a fake. Amber and Oscar were looking around awe-struck too. Oscar was about to go to the kitchen to see what varieties of sandwiches were kept, but Amber pulled him behind. There were ceiling to floor windows which overlooked the vast sea. But as Blake was staring at it, the view changed. He was now looking at a mountain. Bunny seemed to guess Blake's confusion and replied. "The view shifts because the whole place is covered by the haze. The haze is basically like fog, but it can trick your perception. The haze is mainly used by celestial beings to change their form so that half-celestial beings can see them. Otherwise, If you see their true form your brain will sizzle and your body will evaporate." "It's also used to mask portals to their surroundings right?" Said Amber. "Very good." Replied Bunny. "You are very well read." Amber smiled no doubt beaming with pride. "Wait there are other celestial beings?" "Yes there are" replied Bunny. "The main celestial beings who are living today were created by older celestial beings. When the older celestial beings had a huge war, they killed each other. The war was so huge that it formed the earth and everything on it. The main celestial beings were formed from the blood of the older celestial beings. After they were born, The main celestial beings decided to create world harmony and peace. They built their palace and decided to help the world." "Umm...How did they help the world exactly?" said Blake. "Well, they used their powers." Said Bunny "Like there were 5 celestial beings namely- Adonis, Cassandra, Dion and Irene and titan. Well the last one's name was not titan, that was his nick name, but I'm forbidden to say it, because he is stirring, and you never know when he may strike down." "Oh!" said Blake looking at the sea imagining "Titan" coming down riding a chariot and blasting them to ashes. "Anyway." Bunny continued. "Adonis was the leader, he oversaw everything, like political stuff, making decisions, and stuff like that. His power was to keep everything in order; therefore he was the most powerful amongst them. He could immediately blast someone to ashes just by thinking about it. Basically he had the power to turn anything into pure, raw energy. Then came Cassandra, she mostly saw earthly stuff, and she could draw power directly from the earth. Then came Dion, he was aways the dark, mysterious types. He oversaw all the dark stuff in the dark realm. Which was previously the realm of the ancient celestial beings. After their death everything collapsed there. Everything turned dark, and monsters started rising. When Dion went there he sorted up everything, now uses the monsters which previously sprang up there to his wish. The dark realm is essential because it keeps earth going. Because as soon as something on earth dies, it goes to the dark realm so that it can be replenished and be brought back to earth. Irene controls the portals between worlds. She also controls the haze which when properly used by some chosen half-celestials can be extremely deadly. And of course you know titan. He is slowly stirring waiting for to strike vengeance in the whole world. If he rises then he will destroy all worlds and all the portals connecting to it. But on the bright side, if he rises and he will then he will give us prime positions in his army, and he will take us out of this ridiculous dress" Blake looked at Amber, she put her hand in her pocket where her dagger was stored, looking alarmed. Oscar turned his palms into a fist and waited. There was a deadly silence for 10 seconds then Blake cleared his throat and asked "So um, who's side are you on anyway." "Well after what they celestial beings did to me of course not!" Said Bunny "And the titan is offering me a better deal so obviously supporting him." Blake immediately jumped back and drew his sword. Amber pulled out her dagger. And Oscar balled up his fists which started glowing "It was a trap" Oscar grunted "They knew we would come here." "Yes that's right." Said bunny "We got very specific orders from our boss to kill you, and we wouldn't like to break our promise would we." said bunny with an eerie smile stretched across his face. "Your gonna be very sorry." Said Amber "Oh would we." Said bunny he clapped and about a dozen of other bunnies came shuffling in with swords, spears and shields. "Let the fun begin." said Bunny jumping on his toes. And then they charged.

Chapter 19

Blake was irritated.He was having a good day today. He ate some cotton candy, visited New York, his home after a long time but no, Some stupid bunny with a creepy murderous smile and a delight to kill half-celestials wouldn't let him enjoy his day fully. He had to call his stupid rabbit comrades and try to kill them. So Blake retaliated. His sword fighting instincts from camp kicked in, and in no time he was in autopilot, disintegrating one monster after another. He caught a glimpse of Amber and Oscar doing the same, Oscar with his fiery punches and Amber with her deathly dagger skills. The rabbits may have been good fighters in the past, but they were certainly not good now, with their goofy costumes, they stumbled around getting knocked here and about. Blake materialised a disc and threw it on a bunny. The bunny instantly vaporised. He then summoned a disc on which he jumped, twisted in mid-air and slammed a bunny. The bunny fell, and Oscar jumped on him, punching him and instantly disintegrating the bunny. Blake then dodged a striking form one bunny. He used the chair in the living room as a launchpad, He jumped on it and stabbed a bunny.

In no time all bunnies were turned to dust. "Well that was quick." said Amber panting and holding a dagger. She kind of looked scary with that murderous look in her eye and Blake was kind of relieved that she was on his side. Oscars clothes were in tattered, and so was Blake's. But Blake seemed to notice that after Oscar used his glowing fists attack, he seemed to grow a bit more powerful. Like when he used his fists to attack those vampires Oscar could take out only one of them. But now when he used his attack, Oscar could take out a dozen monsters. And his fists glowed brighter too. They headed out towards the room where Alex was sitting. They saw Alex sauntering about the room. He paid no attention to them as if they were no threat to him. Alex looked like a middle aged man. With curly brown hair and grey eyes. He had a pale complexion which contrasted with his bright blue veins popping around his wrist. His veins were a little too bright for a human though. But Blake figured that he was some special kind of half-celestial being or a monster or some immortal guy who wanted to kill them. Alex seemed to read his thoughts "Well, as you guessed I'm not a human but in fact a minor-celestial being. My parents were the titan lord and Alessia. You know about my father, he is slowly stirring and about to fully awaken. Whereas my mom is the maker of magic. She introduced magic to the world. After the great war of the ancient celestial beings. My mom was the only one who could wield the remnants of the powerful magic left by the ancient celestial ones. So my mom was indeed a very powerful person. Not even the major celestial beings want to go into war with my mom." "So your also a wizard." said Amber "Yes that is correct" replied Alex. "Ancient magic wielders are quite rare. People can only wield magic if they are blessed by my mom or if they are her children, that makes me exceptionally powerful. You can't beat me in combat, you only have a slight chance of beating me in a game of chance and trickery." "So what would it be, fighting me in a 1on 1 deathmatch, or playing against me in a game of trickery." "I'd go for the 1on 1 deathmatch, sour face." said Oscar. "I'm gonna beat you so bad that even your own mom won't recognise you." Oscar balled up his fists and had a grim expression on his face. He was stepping forward to punch Alex, but Blake stopped him. Alex was right, they couldn't beat him in a 1 on 1 combat, even if they all tried together to beat him. They wouldn't be close to harming him. Alex radiated a type of powerful aura. He was the son of extremely most powerful celestial beings, titan and Alessia. They didn't want to pick a fight with him. "Well battle you in a game of trickery." Said Blake. Giving a reassuring nod to Oscar and Amber. "Very well then." Said Alex. "Let's proceed." He gave a cold sneer that would make anyone feel like crawling away to a safe hideout away from this guy. He clapped his hands and the world dissolved into itself. Blake found himself standing next to amber and Oscar on a square shaped ground with large pillars on either side. Opposite him standing was Alex. Grinning like a crazy guy who spent his Friday evenings hitting. A bunch of random people and finding that amusing. "So let's begin." said Alex clapping his hands. He waved in the air and immediately two pieces of wood with a bakelite hilt for the grip. Appeared on the floor. "The instructions for this game is very simple." Said Alex " You need to chose one of these pieces of wood, and I will chose the other one, The wood which burns for more time will win. If you win, I will give you directions to the portal which you are looking for. But if I win, I will kill you. Is that fair?" "Here's the catch?" Said Amber "There is always a catch." "Oh yes, there is a catch." Said Alex "One of the pieces of the fire-wood will burn more than the other one. Therefore that one will burn faster. It's a game of chance, like either picking heads or tails. There is no way to know which piece of wood you will get."

"That's fine with me." said Blake stepping into the arena. He picked up a piece of wood and said: "I chose this one." He remembered all the times in school, he did not excel in science, Math or English. He was pretty much an average student. But he was extremely good at problem solving. Each week on Friday, their class would have one block of problem solving skills. To check the children's mental aptitude. Blake would always get highest in that. and one day his principle called Blake's parents and told them personally that Blake exhibited traits of a "Genius."This was another problem solving question, he thought, and he silently prayed to his stars that he should win this game. "Let's begin, shall we" said Blake aloud in a deep confident voice and he even managed to muster a smile. But that smile soon faded when his wooden piece began to blaze. The bake light grip became uncomfortably hot. While his wooden piece was scorching and the flames on it were red-hot. Alex's wood burnt gently. There was only a small flame flickering on it. "You have fallen into my trap." Said Alex with a smile so cold it would have made the flames on Blake's wood dissipate. "I used magic to turn the tables you see, Both the pieces of wood were meant to burn faster, so it didn't matter which one you picked, and as soon as I went to pick the other one." "You used magic to make that other piece of wood disappear, and you took a normal piece of wood with ought us noticing." Said Amber "I knew it! I knew you would use trickery and magic to win this game!" "It's not cheating you see, I simply didn't state in the rules of the game that using magic was not allowed." Alex said grinning. He summoned a thin rope about a meter long which was glowing bright green and was throwing of sparks as soon as it hit the ground. Alex lashed with his rope, aiming for Blake, Blake dodged of the first few strikes but on the third one. The rope hit his leg, it stung like crazy, and Blake was tempted to throw that greenwood and run away, but he noticed that the arena. Blake and Alex were standing on was now levitating above some chasm. Amber and Oscar were on the other end of the room standing on a kind of ledge. The path that connected the ledge and the stadium that Blake had used to climb on the main arena had vanished. Almost as if the arena had read his thoughts and didn't want anyone to escape. Even if Blake tried jumping from the arena to the ledge he doubted he could make the jump and if he fell into the chasm. He would enter the point of no return. He looked at Alex, he was giving Blake a kind of mocking smile that crazy. Psychotic evil scientists gave in movies before blowing up and entire continent or pressing a button which would end human civilisation. Alex laughed "I just love theses arenas, almost every year some stupid pathetic half-celestial being comes and challenges me. They all end up dying. Man this is just so much fun!" said Alex laughing with glee. his eyes glowed bright green for a second. He summoned another rope and lashed it around the stadium, bright sparks flew everywhere. Blake knew that Alex wouldn't leave his wood on the ground and come charging at him. The cold wind around the stadium and the cold tiles would make the flame dissipate. Blake was running out of time. The flame had almost reached the bakelite grip. Alex kept on lashing out his rope. Blake kept on dodging, but it was tough to move with the raging flame on the wood. Alex let out a guttural laugh and swung his rope rapidly at Blake, Blake didn't have time to side-step the strike, so he jumped. The rope curved in a deadly-arc from its flight course and hit Blake on the leg Blake let out a guttural cry and dropped down on the arena. He felt as if his whole life source was draining out from him. Blake heard amber screaming at him to tell him to withdraw from the fight and telling him to come back. But Blake knew he wouldn't be allowed to leave until the fight was over. He was still holding the blazing wooden piece. And then an idea hit him. He slowly rose, shaking. And then he dropped the wood on the tile. Sure, enough. The wood kept on burning, but not for long Blake suspected he had about a minute before the flame reaches the bakelite grip and extinguishes. He concentrated, And two bright glowing discs materialised in his hands. He too only had about a minute before his powers extinguish. Summoning the discs had drained away half of his strength. He was in really bad shape to fight with his powers, any moment now he could fall unconscious. The medics at camp surely wouldn't approve of this. But he had to make the most out of the situation his friends depended on him, heck the whole world depended on him. He couldn't let them down. So he charged, yelling his voice filled with energy, partly cause he hated Alex, partly because he didn't want to let his friends down, and everyone back at camp, hoping that he would save the day, but mostly because his leg wound hurt him a lot.

Chapter 20

Alex clearly didn't expect a fight with Blake, he yelled at him to go back and kept dodging Blake's strikes with his discs. He used some magic to block out the discs, but Blake just materialised new ones. Some discs which he dodged came back spiralling towards him like a Frisbee. Discs were flying everywhere. Alex couldn't move properly because he was holding the wood, he couldn't keep it down because the flame would be extinguished, so he needed to carry it with him. While on the other hand, Blake could keep his wood down because it was burning in great amounts and the extreme warmth of the wood kept the cold from seeping in it.

Blake Stepped on a disc which was coming like a Frisbee, he used it as a launch pad and soared over to Alex (now that he'd done it so many times he kind of became an expert on it). He used the discs which was on his hand and sliced the wood. Immediately the fire extinguished. Alex looked horrified. "You didn't exactly the state in the game rules the magic is not allowed so..." Alex crumpled to dust. Immediately The arena re-attached itself, and Oscar and Amber came sprinting towards Blake. They hugged him and bandaged his wounds. They asked him if he was okay and stuff. They chatted for a little while, and then Amber called out to them. She pointed towards the pile of dust and in the middle of that lay the map which would lead them to the portal where the portal stone was hidden. "Oh my god, It's in Alaska," said Amber reading the map. There were a bunch of weird symbols on the map which looked part Egyptian. Part Ancient Greek and part gibberish. Blake didn't know how amber was reading that map. Amber must have read his expression because she said "This is the language of the celestials. I had to take classes for a year before I could understand this language you will learn it later on in camp. If we get back to camp" Blake was about to ask that if learning this language would give him brownie points in his college application form when he was interrupted. "YOU DID AWESOME." Came a voice behind them Blake pulled out his sword. Amber took out her daggers, and Oscar made a paper plane with the paper which had the location of the portal. "WELL THAT WAS A GREAT JOB BLAKE, YOU GET MEMBERSHIP TO MY RAINBOW SUMMER CAMP!!" A woman materialised next to them, she wore simple jeans and a shirt that read "Rainbows are cool!" her hair was multicoloured well, like a rainbow "I am sorry, forgot to introduce myself" said the women "I am Alexa. I am the minor celestial being of rainbows, I work for Alessia. Alessia sent me here to check on your progress. Well, I know that the portal which is hidden in Alaska. But it would take you more than three days to reach there if you go on your dragon. And well, you have less than three days." "Why do we have less than three days?" Said Blake "Well because the titans army will reach there before you and you won't be able to secure the portal stone. And hence you won't be able to secure the crystal." All of three of them looked glum "But you guys don't need to look sad, Alessia sent me here for a reason, I can open up a rainbow portal which will lead you straight to Alaska" "Wait, so you are telling me now that rainbows are portals." Said Oscar clearly trying hard not to make a joke. "Yes, they are. You see Alessia cannot handle all portals in all dimensions. There are too many. Therefore, she hired me to run the department of rainbow portals. One good thing about rainbow portals is that they are not unpredictable like other normal portals. They take you exactly where you are supposed to go. So Alessia suggested me that I open a rainbow portal. You guys jump into it while flying your dragon and you will reach Alaska in no time!" "wait, if this quest is really important for the fate of all dimensions then why can tall celestial beings help us and fight with us?" Asked Blake. "Well, because we celestial and minor celestial beings are not allowed to intervene in your quests. We can only guide you or help you a little bit, this order was made when the ancient celestial beings were born. It's an order of the universe itself !" Blake liked rainbows, but only to a certain limit. He didn't like plunging into them and then getting transported to another world, but that's exactly what happened to him.

Chapter 22

Blake woke up with a start, and for the tenth time, he didn't wake up in his comfy bed back at home, he woke up on a dragon while plummeting to his death. Which was strange because Dragons can fly, so why was he free falling? His thoughts were sluggish, and his stomach churned, he really shouldn't have had that double layered cheese burger with extra chicken and triple cheese all Oscars fault. He only had suggested him that. "BLAKE GET OFF THE DRAGON NOW!" Blake thought the former rainbow being had been secretly piggy backing on their ride, but he discovered that it was Amber screaming. With a dazed expression, he managed a "wha-what, why?" She pushed him off the Blacklight's back. She jumped with him with Oscar tailing behind them. They were free falling from the sky, with about 60 seconds to impact. They were never going to make it alive.

Then something wonderful happened. Blake's bag opened into a parachute, and so did Oscars and Ambers, and they gradually descended into a…Kingdom, was it? The place surely looked like a majestic palace. Three huge towers surrounded an oversized villa. A lush green garden was situated in between the castle with fountains all over. Blake and Amber landed gracefully in the garden while Oscar's parachute got stuck on one of the fountains and Oscar was dangling helplessly a few feet above the ground. "A little help," said Oscar. "Should we just leave him like this" said Amber "Nah, we need someone to cook food, but we can do this." Blake pulled out his I-Phone which was slightly cracked from all the adventures he had, he took a photo of Oscar and then put it back in his pocket. It took a while to remove Oscar, but they managed it. 2 security guards stopped them.

Amber explained to them that they were here to meet kind Icarus for some diplomatic reasons. She needed to fill some forms for crossing different dimensions and stuff, but after some time the guards took them inside the villa. The villa was filled with unique paintings, antique objects and overpriced rugs. There were several Lamborghini's and BMW's parked outside the villa. The flooring of the villa was Italian marble with gold plated walls. It was a hundred times better than Alex's ship. They were led into a room where U-shaped thrones were carved around, advisors were seated all around. At the centre of the U there was an oversized throne decorated with rare gems and on top of that sat king Icarus.

Blake could tell he was king Icarus because he wore a t-shirt which said: "That's Right, I am King Icarus!!" And he wore a platinum crown with the initials "KC" carved on it, which meant King Icarus

Blake guessed. "Well, well." said Icarus " I have been expecting you, Blake." After so many encounters with psychotic, murderous, crazy celestial beings. Blake knew that if someone knows your name and is expecting you it either means good news or bad news. With Blake's luck he knew it would be bad news. "You see all celestial beings are a big family, word got around that you are the chosen one, and I knew that you would be here Because you want that location to that Portal stone" said Icarus "Whose side are you on?" Said Blake. "I really haven't picked sides in this war you see, I want to be on the winning side, so ill wait until the last moment to pick sides, I will give you the location if you do something for me in return" Blake hated this part the most, whenever you wanted a favour from one of these guys they always told you to go on a fatal quest to retrieve something lost, or stolen or forgotten or something like that. "It's simple." Said Icarus "You need to retrieve the ancient throne which was stolen centuries ago by giants. Also you have just 8 hours to do this, the map to the place will be provided by my advisors." He pointed out towards several bored looking advisors, some were snoring away to glory while others were clipping their nails or reading the papers. "Did the titan's army come here, before us." Asked Blake "No they didn't, but they still might know where the location is, so you better hurry." said Icarus. Blake nodded. "Well who is ready for another terrifying and fatal quest," asked Oscar Blake and Amber groaned. Oscar sure had a way to lift peoples spirits up.

Chapter 23

Surprisingly, the giants' lair was not far away, it was maybe a one-drive if you were going by car, but they were going by a flying

So they reached the place in about 15 miniutes. The giants lair was in-fact a huge evergreen forest. Lush bushes surrounded the forest on all sides. It was pretty tough to get inside the forest because the whole surrounding was lined up with traps. Sinkholes and thick branches, but they managed. They found a small hut in the centre of the forest, the hut was surrounded by huge oak fences, as soon as they came close to the fence, the oak trees started burning a purple flame, they could hear a faint pulse which was rippling through the air. And then a giant emerged from the hut. The giant was huge, he was as tall as three men put together with the width of a bulldozer. The giant had a scaly, green reptilian skin. And his head was of a goat. Not the normal type of goat though, his horns curled up behind his head so much they touched the base of his skull. "I know why you are here, I know what you came looking for, but first you must beat theses oak fences, only then we can negotiate," said the giant in a deep, resonating voice. With that he went inside his hut. The purple flames were still dancing on top of the oak, and if they approached it, they would start to burn more, and the pulsing sound would increase. Amber tried throwing her daggers into the oak tree, no luck, they just sank in the oak and disappeared.

Blake threw one of his discs on the oak, it just passed the tree as if it was made of air. Then at last Oscar sat up and said "Well, I guess I know how to break theses oak fences" He went near the fence, his hands started to blaze, and he dipped his hand into the fire. Blake thought Oscar had officially lost it, he and Amber ran towards Blake to help pull him back, but then suddenly the oak fences exploded, throwing Blake and amber behind. Oscar was doused with purple flames. After Blake and Amber got up, they ran towards Oscar. Nothing happened to Oscar, purple flames still surrounded him, but he was pretty much intact. Oscar closed his wrist, immediately the purple flames raced down his wrist into his hands and died out. Blake and Amber looked bewildered. They heard clapping behind Oscar. Oscar looked behind, and he saw the giant, "At last, a half-celestial blessed by Adonis himself." Said the giant. And then disappeared inside the hut.Oscar promptly collapsed.

After giving Oscar some golden water, and healing him, Amber and Blake headed inside the hut with Oscar who was leaning against Blake. They sat on the couches beside the fireplace. The hut was medium sized with a dining table and another room. The giant sat in the centre "He must be tired controlling the flames." said the giant. Oscar just nodded. "What did you mean by that he is blessed by Adonis himself?" "Adonis someday knew that the prophecy of doom is going to come again." Said the giant. "Therefore he blessed one of the half-celestial beings to have a part of his power, that is to harness raw, pure energy from the environment. Oscar does this by channeling energy into himself, that is how he could take out the oak trees? He harnessed their power. This has only been done a couple of times in the past, It's sporadic that Adonis grants this power to half-celestial beings. The last time he gave this power to a half-celestial, the half-celestial caused many problems." "Like what?" Said Amber "Well, he first sided with the Titan, and then when they lost he was taken to imperial prison in the celestial realm. He was released 5 years back and told to live as a mortal. But then he blew up 43 ships of the army. Which was carrying some top-secret weapon? And also a half-celestial being. The army took years to recover that weapon and the half-celestial was never found." Blake and Amber looked aghast. "But you guys don't need to worry, I'm sure Oscar won't blow up anything."

Said the giant. Oscar gave a thumbs up sign while nibbling on a sandwich he had safely stored in his backpack. "And about the Lost Throne. It's in the backyard you can take it while you are leaving." Said the Giant. "And who are you?" Asked Amber. "I was in the army of the celestials; I will once again fight in the final battle. But for now, I am here."

They thanked the giant and headed out towards the throne. The throne was surprisingly light, and Blake could easily lift it, and he carried it like a backpack. Amber explained that the throne was extremely light yet very durable because it was made from an alloy of chromium and copper. Blake thanked God that he luckily didn't sign up for the monthly program of classifying metals and stating their uses because he never would have made it alive if that's what they learnt. They reached the palace with still 6 hours on the clock, they were surprisingly early. They handed over the throne to Icarus who was apparently watching T.V he told one of his advisors to take it into the storage room and dump it. This made Blake angry because They had really worked hard to get the throne, Oscar had risked his life to put out the flames. But Blake didn't show it, they just needed the map to the portal stone, and then they could return to camp safely. "The map will be given to you by my advisors, you must be tired so rest here tonight, and leave first thing in the morning" Blake didn't want to rest here, he didn't trust Icarus but as soon as he had said sleep Blake wanted to collapse and sleep like a log. And plus Amber and Oscar needed rest to even they were tired. They headed towards their rooms and as soon as Blake's head hit the pillow, he zoned out. Blake woke up refreshed and recharged the next day. They quickly had their breakfast, and the advisors gave them the map, Amber started to read it, and she gasped. "What happened?" Asked Blake "It says here that the location of the the portal stone is in the dark realm." said Amber "But mortals can't get inside the dark realm, we will disintegrate." said Oscar. "That is what the potion you got from the mountain of Doom is for." said one of the advisors. "The potion will protect you from the side effects of the portal stone, and it will let you pass into the dark realm unnoticed." Blake nodded. "Well then let's go and bring back a portal stone" said Blake they all nodded looking determined.

Chapter 24

Blake was bored out of his mind. He aimlessly sauntered around the park while Amber tried to figure out where the portal to the dark realm was located. Oscar was sitting and munching a sandwich. That guy just loved sandwiches. "According to the map, the portal must be here," said Amber pointing to a pile of rocks. "Well we need a portal opener to figure this out," said Oscar unpacking yet another sandwich. Where did this guy store so many sandwiches? Blake thought. "What is a portal opener?" Said Blake "Did you not attend any classes in camp?" Said Amber. Blake recalled playing Fifa at camp, but he doubted if that would be counted as a class. "A portal opener is basically a type of key any half-celestial or celestial being can summon which would grant him cases to any portal. But with portals such as the dark realm, only advanced magic would summon such a key," said Amber. "Then do it, summon a portal opener." said Blake "I can't, I don't know how to" said Amber "Did you not attend any classes at camp?" said Blake Amber rolled her eyes. "Well, I do remember one thing I learnt at the portal lecture." Said Blake "Portals are really delicate right, so maybe we can conjure enough energy to break the portal, and as soon as that happens, we jump into it, so when the portal collapses, we reach the dark realm." "Theoretically, it is possible but also dangerous" said Amber "It's worth a shot" said Blake. "I am ready." Said Oscar.

Blake Concentrated hard, he waited for a couple of moments, and then a concentrated beam of energy erupted from his hands and hit the rock. The rock didn't erupt or vanish like other normal rocks, instead it began steaming, and smoldering. Changing different hues of blood red and orange. Wisps of smoke began to rise form the rocks, and Bike could see that the entire landscape was rippling, like when you throw a rock in still water. "Amber now!" Said Blake. Amber thrust her hand forward and a tendrils of red energy began wrapping itself around the rocks. Basically their plan was to break the rocks so that the portal would be revealed and then they could jump in it. Blake was concentrating his power into the rocks. While Amber would make sure that the energy stays in one place and the whole thing does not erupt. Oscar would then go and break the rocks with his fists. Their timing had to be perfect, or else they would disintegrate and end up gods know where. "Oscar go!" Yelled Amber. Their powers would exhaust any minute now, they had to break the portal fast. Oscar went near the rocks, for some reason Oscar could absorb some energy. So even if he went close to a high source of energy it won't affect him that much. It could do some harm, but this was important.

Oscar balled up his fists and concentrated. His fists started to glow bright orange with a yell he smashed his fist into the ground. The ground rippled as if It's was made of water, the rocks began glowing bright "JUMP IN!" yelled Amber. The all charged into the rocks, as the ground started swirling, and then they evaporated.

Blake didn't believe his eyes. He thought the dark realm was dark, scary with dangerous beasts lurking around, but what he saw was completely different. They were in a cavern with walls that were made of bedrock. But it was different than the normal bedrock because it was swirling with a reddish pattern. Just by looking at it, made Blake dizzy. The floors were covered with some type of transparent glass, underneath that there was dark smoke hissing against the floor. "This part of the dark realm is not directly under Dion's control. He only access it sometimes." Said Amber. "I really am not feeling that good." Said Oscar, his skin a tinge of blue. "Maybe using your powers would have exhausted you." Said Amber. Even Blake was feeling tired, his eyelids were turning heavy. Amber yawned. "Oh my god, we forgot to drink the potion, with ought it our essence will fade away." She furiously started digging through her pouch. Blake knew he was in trouble. His hands were turning transparent and as soon as he touched them to the ground they hissed. But he couldn't concentrate. His legs turned to jelly, he sat down while Oscar just collapsed. He forgot all about his mission, his mind was drifting away. He was slowly closing his eyelids. Just then he felt that someone had just doused him with acid, his hands hands burnt. He opened his eyes and saw that a black liquid was running down his forehead. The liquid then suddenly evaporated. He felt better, as if he was just about to float away and someone had placed an anchor to hold him to the ground. He looked at Amber, she was slowly getting up with an empty vial in her hand. Oscar too woke up, his skin colour started to return.

"I poured the vials on you just before you guys started to fade away." Said Amber. The black liquid on her forehead was also starting to evaporate. Blake got up, "Well then lets find that portal stone and get out of here." said Blake. They all agreed, they didn't want to stick around in this place a minute longer than they actually had to.

They searched for about 30 minutes, Blake was just about to go and take a break when Amber called "Hey guys, I think I found something." Blake and Oscar hurried towards Amber. She pointed towards a chunk of rock in the centre of the wall, unlike the shade of the wall, this rock glowed bright orange. "How are we gonna take that chunk of rock out? its wedged right in the centre of the wall."Said Blake "Well, I could try to take it out with my punches" said Oscar his fists glowing."No, the energy you will exert when you punch the stone, might come back at you with even more energy, because this stone is unstable, and it might kill you, let's try my method." Said Amber. She summoned three daggers and handed them one each. "We will break the wall around the stone so that we can take it out," said Amber. They trio go to work.

Chapter 25

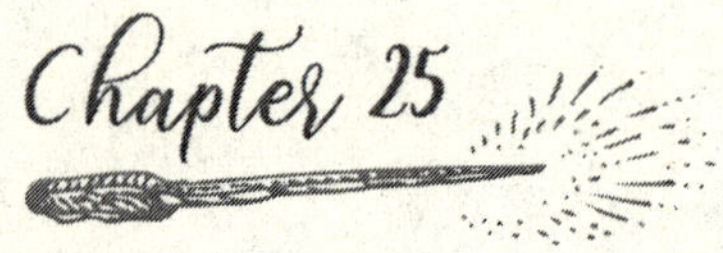

After about 15 minutes they were done, Amber pulled out the final piece, and the stone came to lose. Amber pulled it out with a look of surprise on her face. The rock glowed a contrast of orange and yellow. Ancient text millennium old was inscribed on it. "I think a great sacrifice was made here, it says that the monsters in this dimension were about to come into other dimensions, but a brave soldier sacrificed his life so that the monsters could never reach the upper world," said Amber reading the ancient text. "Well now let's get out of here." Said Blake. "I don't think so." Said a man behind them. He wore a mask with various scars embedded on his face. His eyes were the color of emeralds. "I am formerly known as the Titan, and I have got very specific orders to kill you."

Normally Blake didn't get death threats that often, but this week he had got almost 15. Almost any person Blake encountered in this dimension wanted to kill him. He wanted to go to the normal earth where the only "Threats!" he got was his teacher telling him to do his H.W or else she would call his parents. "But how is this possible, the bunny said you are stirring, and you are not yet fully awake." Blake blurted out. "That is true, I am yet not fully awake, this form is a mere projection of my true self." said Titan his form flickering "But this form is enough to kill you." "Nah I'm not in a mood, come next week, or how about NEVER," said Blake. The Titan lunged at Blake with a glinting, wicked sharp sword in his hands. Even for a projection, Titan could move incredibly fast, fortunately, Blake had practiced dodging strikes. He sidestepped and jabbed his own blade on the back of the Titan, but the Titan expected his attack. He twisted parried Blake's strike and kicked Blake's hand. The kick had enough force to topple Blake's sword. The sword fell out of Blake's hand and skidded on the floor. Blake stood defenseless before the Titan, a drop of sweat trickling down his forehead. This was the end, he knew it. He would never return back to earth. He was too far away to grab the sword. Even if he tried Titan would be fast enough to strike him down with his blade. Just then the unexpected happened. Blake saw a flying sandwich in slow-motion coming. It may have been that Blake was so shocked that his brain was processing information very slowly. The Titan was too busy laughing with glee, the sandwiches projectile course was aimed at the Titan's head, Blake lunged onto another side as the Titan struck with his sword. The strike could have easily hit Blake and decimated him, but the sandwich hit the Titan's face first, and he couldn't make out where Blake was, Blake rolled and stood up, the Titan's sword had missed Blake by a hairs width. "WHO

DARES TO HIT THE LORD OF ETERNAL DARKNESS WITH A...Chicken grilled sandwich with extra lettuce and triple cheese." Said the Titan gulping. Blake looked at Oscar, he had immediate earned Blake's permanent respect by hitting the lord of eternal darkness with a...Sandwich. "Even though the sandwich is quite good" said the Titan taking a huge bite. "I WILL STILL KILL YOU!!" said the Titan running at lightning speed towards Oscar. Oscar had a panicked look on his face; he jumped onto the other side just when Amber thrust her hand forward. Enormous rope's like the one's Alex used materialised and wrapped themselves around the Titans hands, legs, and waist. He struggled to break free just then Oscar came sprinting towards the Titan. His hands glowing; he sidestepped and punched the Titan on the face. The Titan's form flickered. But the Titan quickly recovered he grabbed Oscar by the wrist and threw him in the direction of Amber. Even in only a projection form the Titan was ridiculously powerful. Amber didn't see Oscar coming towards her like a comet. Oscar crashed into Amber. The ropes dematerialised.

Blake ran and summoned his discs, he Threw one at Titan, the Titan dodged it easily but the disc came hurling back at him like a Frisbee, The Titan Didn't expect this attack. It him on the back, but he simply winced and knelt down. It would take more than a couple of discs to take down this guy. He rushed towards Amber and Oscar. They both were fine, they just had a few minor cuts "Do you remember Blake how you saved us during the camp games." Said Amber "Yeah, I used an ancient statue which gave off a lot of energy to charge my powers." "Exactly, do they same thing, use this century old cavern, you don't need the crystal to give you powers, you already have them inside you." Said Amber Blake nodded "We need to do the same thing we did to break the portal, we need to work together to bring this guy down." Said Blake. Oscar and Amber nodded. "Well…Well. Are you done with you little team planning, believe me, its going to take more than a couple of half-celestials to bring me down. Even in my projection form I am still called THE LORD OF ETERNAL DARKNESS." Amber struck first, she threw one of her daggers at the Titan. He dodged, Blake summoned levitating discs, as soon as he jumped over one, another disc would materialise, so Blake was basically running on air, Oscar and Amber ran towards the Titan. The were cornering him from all three sides, Amber was continuously throwing daggers at him to distract him while Oscar started furiously hitting him with punches. Blake started striking him down with his sword, Even though all three of them were attacking, they were no-match for him. He continuously dodged all their strikes, and attacked, soon they were tired. The Titan thrust his hand forward a inky black beam of current shot from his hand and hit Oscar. Amber rushed towards him but the Titan summoned another beam and knocked Amber of her feet. Only Blake was left. The Titan turned his attention towards Blake, "A special attack for my honored guest." A thrust his hand forward and a beam of green glowing energy, ten times more powerful than the last one's shot towards Blake.

Chapter 26

Blake knew how it was going to end, his gravestone would say instead of "Rest in piece." His gravestone would say "rest in pieces" or maybe, the blast would be so powerful his body would just disintegrate. But his friends were counting on him, he couldn't let them down, so he summoned a dozen of discs on his hand, one behind the other and held it like a shield. He also summoned a disc directly behind him, he hoped this plan would work. As soon as the blast hit his shield the first three disintegrated, but the blast was so powerful, it sent him flying on the disc he had summoned earlier. His plan had worked, he knew that the blast would be extremely powerful and he wouldn't be able to hold his ground, the the disc behind him had acted like a cushion so he wouldn't go flying behind hitting the rocks. If it wasn't for the disc behind him he would have disintegrated completely. "A great plan, but let's see if you can execute it under dire conditions." The intensity of the beam increased. The disc Blake held together like a shield, started slowly disintegrating one by one, he just had 7 discs left now. His back started crushing on the disc behind him. He was slowly being squashed, Summoning the discs had cost a lot on his energy. He was tired and he was being sandwiched between a disc which was meant to act like a cushion and a death ray which would vanish him on contact. His friends lay sprawling on the floor slowly trying to get up even if his friends got up, they would be too late to save him. The odds of winning the fight were not that great. Then he remembered what Amber had said about the cavern being ancient, and full of energy. He could feel the energy buzzing all around him. This was a place where energy of the world got replenished, this cave was a part of a place where life was made. And then he finally understood it, his power was giving other things energy. Giving them power. That is why he felt so powerful around stuff that was about to give off a lot of energy like a volcano or something in which great energy had been deposited. This whole cavern was brimming with energy because a great sacrifice was made, the half-celestial had given his energy to this cavern. And now it was time to return back the energy. Blake closed his eyes he concentrated and then he yelled and pushed the discs in front of him. Immediately a cloud of blue smoke started to rise from his feet. And then a huge beam of energy raced from his hands down to his fingertips and fired towards the Titan, apparently Blake's beam was more powerful. It hit the Titan right in the centre of chest and he went crashing behind into the wall. The Titans form started flickering, green light started spilling out of his chest. He slowly got up, wincing, Blake was feeling tired. His joints hurt and he could barely stand, dark spots danced in front of him. He wheezed, his adrenaline was wearing away, and summoning that beam of energy had made him extremely tired. He was going to collapse any second now. The Titan slowly limped with a sword in his hand and started advancing. Blake held up his sword. And then the Titans eye widened, he started down at his chest. It started steaming and then he collapsed, behind him was standing Oscar, with his fists advanced and glowing. Blake went near the Titan "This has not ended Blake, I will come again, in my new form, and you will be sorry." Said The Titan. Blake held up his sword and then drove it straight through the Titans heart. The titan exploded in a violent explosion sending green light everywhere. And Oscar and Blake went flying hitting the wall. Oscar groaned and got up. Blake lay unconscious over the floor. The cavern started collapsing and Amber yelled "We need to get out of here!"

"Will Blake be okay?" Asked Oscar, they were flying on their dragon and had successfully got out of the cavern before it collapsed. They had also got the portal stone, Blake lay strapped unconscious on the dragon. Amber had done some basic healing on him, but he still hadn't woken up. Amber had reassured him that Blake will be alright. But Oscar couldn't shake out the feeling that the Titan had said something about someone he was serving. And he had said that he would return. They were going back to camp, but their mission wasn't over yet.

Chapter 21

Blake thought that the camp would be livelier after he successfully returned From the mission securing the portal stone and defeating a form of the Titan. He secretly hoped that they would hang banners around the camp with something like "Welcome back Blake, Your our HERO." or something like that. Well, he was wrong. The campers were congratulating him, and patting him on the back and everything, but they seemed tensed. Like it was the calm before the storm. This made Blake uneasy. He knew something was up so he decided to go to ask his mentor, Master Domo. "Well, we are really happy that you secured the portal stone but that means that now the real war has begun." said Master Domo "I don't understand." Said Blake, Master Domo sighed and Blake kind of heard him saying "When do you understand." Under his breath, but he ignored it. "Well, that means that as soon as you secured the portal stone. The prophecy of the big war started. We knew it was coming but now since you got that stone, its confirmed, and the other two chosen ones are Amber and Oscar, you may have guessed this." "Oh." Blake responded. "And another thing." Said Blake "The way Titan was talking it was looking like even he has a master, do you know who it could be." "Well, maybe he was just trying to play with your mind, or maybe there is someone out there who he is serving, but that entity must be extremely powerful that Titan himself has gone under his command, as of now I don't know wether such a being exists." Blake nodded, he thanked Master Domo and headed out towards the barbecue, there was at- least something good in the world.

They chatted around the campfire and sang together. Everyone was in a good mood. He at a colossal dinner and headed out towards his bunker, as soon as his head hit the pillow he fell asleep, but unfortunately, dreams found him. He was a cavern in some sorts, with a huge abyss in the middle. Red hot steam rose from the chasm and stung his face. The whole place was lined up with broken shelves and ancient old artifacts. Sentry guards stood all around the place, some were giants while others were monsters. But there were also a few who were human. He looked down, and he almost had a fit. It was looking like he was made of steam, he could see through himself. And the other guards couldn't see him. A guard passed through him, and that gave Blake vertigo. He approached a throne made of ivory and silver at the edges. There was a massive person sitting on top of the throne towering a man with sea green eyes and a mask with scars. Blake gnashed his teeth, it was Titan. "I am sorry sir, my form had not recuperated properly. I need rest." said Titan his voice trembling with fear. "I told you to do bring one dam...Crystal and fight an amateur group, you could do that in any form!" said the man on the throne. Blake tried to get a closer look at the guy on the throne but as soon as he stepped closer to the throne, his form shimmered. Blake thought it was best to maintain his distance or else Titan or the man on the throne would be able to sense his presence. The man on the throne was wearing some type helmet which covered his face, he wore armor which was polished with gold. Anyone his size would not be human Blake thought. He could be a giant, but that guy radiated a sort of death and fear aura so strong. Blake wanted to run away and get one of those rocket launchers to defend himself. But he doubted even that would do any good against this guy. "Well, I have already put someone else for this job, he is one of them only but he works for us." said the man on the throne. "Smart sir." replied Titan. "But to invade their camp you would need the fallen cloak and the cursed shield to use their magic against them."Said Titan "That will be handled by the spy, he will reach the camp by tomorrow, he is a special guest. No one will suspect him." Said the person on the throne. Then Titan froze, he looked behind, directly at Blake.He took out his sword in a second and slashed at Blake, the dream dissolved. Blake woke up gasping. He could almost feel the edges of the blade on his throat. Then he heard shouting outside he immediately raced down his bunker in his pajamas and opened the door, everybody was shouting and cheering and waving banners that read "Welcome back." A man on a sky coloured dragon, he had golden hair and sky blue eyes, he stepped down gracefully from the dragon as if this was his everyday job and shook hands with people, "That's marquee." A guy whispered to him behind, he is one of the special guests, others are coming by next week. Blake stared at the crowd in horror. He kept remembering his dream That will be handled by the spy, he will reach the camp by tomorrow. He is a special guest. No one will suspect him the man on the throne had said. And then he rushed to Master Domo, because he knew only he would believe Blake.